D0824987

Vincent Silva

Senso Owari

(The War Is Ended)

SGT Vincent Silva

Survivor
*World War II, Bataan Death March,
3½ years Prisoner of War of Japan*

WITHDRAWN

AuthorHouse™
1663 Liberty Drive, Suite 200
Bloomington, IN 47403
www.authorhouse.com
Phone: 1-800-839-8640

© 2008 SGT Vincent Silva. All rights reserved.

www.TheWarIsEnded.com

No part of this book may be reproduced, stored in a retrieval system, or transmitted by any means without the written permission of the author.

First published by AuthorHouse 2/26/2008

ISBN: 978-1-4343-6462-3 (sc)

Library of Congress Control Number: 2008901117

Printed in the United States of America
Bloomington, Indiana

This book is printed on acid-free paper.

Letter to the Reader

Invincible: Incapable of being conquered, overcome, or subdued.

During the many hours I spent working with my father on this manuscript, I discovered a man I now know to be truly invincible. This story is not just a history of my father and my family, it is the history of some of the darkest days of my country. Author/Anchorman Tom Brokaw refers to the men and women of my parents' era as "The Greatest Generation." I now understand what it takes to be the greatest generation. It takes men and women who are invincible.

This is a book of the memories of my father as they were told to me. I have written them to preserve the details of his life for his children and his children's children. No human should ever experience what my father endured during his captivity. Untold numbers of American and Filipino soldiers died under the almost constant torture and brutal living conditions in the Japanese prisoner of war camps. My father did not die. His courage and sheer will to survive proved to be stronger than the relentless suffering he endured. He never lost hope, and he never faltered in his belief that he would someday return home to his family. We, his children, are thankful for the man we call Papa.

I could not have completed this book without the help of my cousin Tommy Baca. His guidance and editing skills proved to be essential. His abundance of family pictures and knowledge of family history added color and insight to this story.

A great big heartfelt thank you goes out to Jean Georgakopoulos. She thought she had retired from her high school English teaching chores. Not so—I brought her back from retirement. I found her red ink pen to be just as sharp as always. If you, the reader, happen across a typo, misspelling, or extra comma, you can give blame to Jean.

I am grateful to another survivor of the Death March and Japanese prison camp, Mr. Ben Steele. He gave me permission to print one of his drawings from his memory of the Death March. You will find this drawing on page 23. Thank you Mr. Steele.

Last but not least, I must say thanks to my husband and my best friend, Chuck Cannon. You provided me with encouragement and guidance. With your help my dream became a reality. Thanks and I love you Sugarboy.

Penny Silva Cannon

Dedication

In memory of my loving wife, Rose, and our youngest son, Richard Silva.

To my children,
Linda Gregoire, Penny Cannon, Dr. Vincent A. Silva, Jr., and Marjorie Rose Silva.

To my grandchildren,
Corie Gregoire, Roger Gregoire III, Kimberly Huffman, Kristina Silva, Vincent Anthony Silva, Robert Lee Silva, and Michael Silva.

To my great-grandchildren,
Robert Camacho, Mark Camacho, Rikki Gregoire, Kristen Gregoire, Roger Gregoire IV, Brittney Rose Gregoire, Monique Rose Silva Crossman, Vincent Andrés Silva, Arianna Silva, Taylor Rose Silva, Andrew Silva, and Natalia Silva.

And my great-great granddaughter,
Tiana Gregoire

Preface

The closet was filled with my mother's clothes. The chest continued to hold all her belongings. The cabinet in the bathroom claimed all the many medicine bottles with her name on them.

Two days had passed since the funeral. The out of town relatives had all gone home. My legally blind father was now living alone.

My sisters and I, along with other family members, had taken turns this last month staying day and night with my mother and father. We were there to see that all their needs were met and now to keep my father company.

The weather was unusually warm for December as my dad and I sat outside on the balcony. This had been my mom's favorite place of their third floor apartment, the last home my mom and dad shared together. They had sold the family home in February of that same year and moved into a large, one-bedroom apartment at Quail Lodge, a "gracious living retirement community" as described in the Quail Lodge brochure.

It was hard at first for my father to adjust to living in an apartment after having his own home for so many years. For him it was too confining and claustrophobic. This was not the case for my mother. She loved the freedom. No more cooking three meals a day. No more shopping and washing dishes. She loved the food the chef at Quail Lodge prepared. She even gained some weight. She made friends with the other residents and she seemed to have more energy. Even though she had been diagnosed with cancer (which was the main reason for moving the two of them into Quail Lodge), it appeared to all of us that she was thriving in her new environment. It was only in the last four weeks of her life that the cancer consumed her. First it took away her energy and then her body.

"Dad is it OK with you if I start packing up mom's clothes?"

I don't know where his thoughts were but I don't think he was ready to leave them because it took him some time to respond to my question.

"She has some really nice clothes. She always took great care in how she looked. Do you think anyone in the family will want her clothes?"

"Dad she was a size 6. No one in the family is that small." I could see the disappointment in his eyes.

I immediately responded with, "You're right, Dad. We should all take something of mom's to remember her."

Her purses and her jewelry had already been lovingly divided among us girls. In going through her purses we discovered over two thousand dollars she had hidden away. This was her so-called "Mad Money." If any of her children or grandchildren needed money, she was the one we went to. If one of us took her out to lunch or dinner, which she loved to do, she always insisted that it was her treat. If she had an offer to go to Lake Tahoe, she was ready. On most trips to the casinos, my mom was most likely the only one walking out with her winnings.

That day I started the task of going through her closet. The discovery I made in a box at the back of her closet was far more valuable then all of her "Mad Money." In this box, along with old photos and old letters, was a collection of old newspaper articles.

I knew that my father had years before written a number of newspaper articles describing his life in the military during WWII. I had even read one or two. This box contained the full collection of every article.

And so began my journey into my Father's past.

Table of Contents

Chapter 1: Before the War

Chapter 2: World War II

Chapter 3: The Surrender of Bataan

Chapter 4: The Bataan Death March

Chapter 5: Camp O'Donnell

Chapter 6: Camp Cabanatuan

Chapter 7: The Noto Maru

Chapter 8: Life in Japan

Chapter 9: Liberation

Chapter 10: Homecoming

Chapter 11: Civilian Life

A.   Awards and Citations

B.   Family Tree

C.   Poems by Vincent Silva

D.   Additional Information

List of Figures

Chapter 1: Before the War

Chapter 2: World War II

Chapter 3: The Surrender of Bataan

Chapter 4: The Bataan Death March

Chapter 5: Camp O'Donnell

Chapter 6: Camp Cabanatuan

Chapter 7: The Noto Maru

Chapter 8: Life in Japan

Chapter 9: Liberation

Chapter 10: Homecoming

Chapter 11: Civilian Life

A.   Awards and Citations

B.   Family Tree

C.   Poems by Vincent Silva

D.   Additional Information

Chapter 1: Before the War

Early Years

I was born April 12, 1918, on my family's cattle ranch, El Rancho del Coyote or the Ranch of the Coyote. The ranch was near the small village of Las Golondrinas, about thirty miles north of the city of Las Vegas, New Mexico. The ranch has been in my family since 1765 when the King of Spain gave it to the Silva family through a Spanish Land Grant. The 5000-acre ranch is in a beautiful valley with rich virgin soil. There is a river that flows through our ranch called El Río del Coyote (the Coyote River). We always had plenty of good fresh water. We had a large comfortable home with thick adobe walls for both insulation as well as protection against Indian attacks. The Apache raids continued even into the twentieth century. Family members still live on the ranch today.

My father and mother, Leandro (Lee)[1] Silva and Beatriz (Beatrice)[2] Romero Silva, moved from the family ranch to the coal camp of Swastika, New Mexico, in 1926 when I was eight years old. They did this so my father could work in the mines and their children could go to public school. My mother's older brother Frank Romero[3] and his family also lived in Swastika at the time. Uncle Frank was a veteran of the Spanish American War. He served under Teddy Roosevelt in the Philippines and in Cuba.

After the swastika became associated with Adolf Hitler and the Nazi Party, the name of our coal camp was changed from Swastika to Brilliant. I have no idea why anyone working in the black depths of a coal mine would name the town "Brilliant."

---

1. Leandro Silva, January 20, 1898 - February 12, 1960.

2. Beatriz Romero Silva, September 18, 1899 - February 26, 1976.

3. Filadelfio (Frank) Romero, (1885-1969). She had a younger half-brother, Francisco (Frank) Romero (1907-1995) who lived in Pueblo, Colorado.

Figure 1-1: Lee, Beatrice, and Vincent Silva, circa 1920

Coal Camps

My early memories are full of family and friends in this small coal mining camp in northeastern New Mexico. My Uncle Frank and Aunt Rachel[4], with their six boys and one girl, lived across the street from us. Uncle Frank was the town constable. One day my sister's little dog went into the neighbor's yard. The neighbor got so mad that he threw the dog into the street and killed

---

4. Rachel (Raquela) Romero (1895-1979)

it. My Uncle Frank, "The Town Constable," threw the neighbor in jail for the night. My uncle was also the Boy Scout leader for our community. He provided us boys with countless camping and hunting trips.

Figure 1-2: Vincent Silva in Swastika, NM, circa 1928

I am a child of the Great Depression and Prohibition. My dad and Uncle Frank had a small family business that I helped out with. My dad and uncle purchased grapes that came into town by train from California. The grapes were put into large tubs and my cousin, Pat Romero, and I had the job of crushing the grapes. The first crush was the best quality and that was always placed in oak barrels and saved in our cellar for special occasions. The juice that was left after the second crush was also saved. It was cleaned and strained and then distilled in copper kettles and copper tubing into a fine whiskey. The juice from the second crush was sold as medicine.

During the Depression years, the mines were worked only one day a week. It was hard for my mom and dad to feed and clothe three children[5]. We lived in a comfortable home, which was owned by the St. Louis, Rocky Mountain, and Pacific Company. We always had good healthy meals and a loving family to

5. Leandro and Beatriz Silva had two additional children, Bernardino and Georgina, who died as infants.

care for us. My sister Juaquinita, my brother Henri, and I spent most of our summers on the ranch with our grandparents, aunts, uncles, and lots of cousins. There were always lots of fresh vegetables from the garden, milk and cheese from the dairy cows, and fresh meat from butchered livestock.

The summer of 1931 was most memorable. I was 13, old enough to help herd the sheep from our ranch in Las Golondrinas (the Swallows) to Agua Caliente (Hot Water). This was a natural hot water spring about sixty miles from our ranch. It was believed that the waters from the spring had healing powers and that the sheep, after bathing in the warm water would be free from disease for the next year. At night we would sleep under the wagon which carried our food and supplies. My Uncle Baltazar Mares[6] was the camp cook. He would build an open fire and prepare our meals over the hot embers. The food was good but the adventure was priceless.

I received a very good education in the small community of Brilliant. While in the eighth grade, I participated in the state spelling bee which was held in Santa Fé, New Mexico. I brought home a certificate for fourth place in this competition. When it was time for me to attend high school, I entered Ratón High. This was the closest high school in Colfax County, about seven miles away in the town of Ratón. At eighteen, I left high school so that I could work with my father in the coal mines.

Meeting and Marrying Rose

After working a few months in the mines, I had saved enough money to buy a 1934 V-8 Ford. This is every young man's dream, even back in the dark ages of 1936.

Figure 1-3: 1934 V-8 Ford

---

6. No relation to Frank and Luisa Mares.

I was free to drive with my friends into town to see a movie or go to one of the many town dances. One trip in particular lives vividly in my memory. It was Thanksgiving Day 1937. My buddy John Trujillo and I had gone into town to watch the Ratón Tigers, our high school football team, play the Dawson[7] Miners. After the game, we decided to drive through town. As we were driving past the city park, I saw Pauline Quintana, a girl that I knew. She was a friend of my sister. With her was the most beautiful girl I had ever seen. Without hesitation I stopped the car and walked to where they were. My sister's friend Pauline introduced me to the girl with her. She was her cousin Rose Mares. I took one look at this beautiful girl and immediately knew that she was the girl I was going to marry. I did not want to lose her, so I followed her home. I knocked at the front door, and introduced myself to her father, Francisco Mares[8], when he answered the door. If I had known at the time that Mr. Mares was the county sheriff I may not have been so bold. After that introduction Rose and I started dating.

It was the tradition for the parents of the young man to go to the home of the young woman and ask her parents on behalf of their son for permission to marry their daughter. On the appointed day my mom and dad, along with my Uncle Frank and Aunt Rachel, accompanied me to the Mares' home. We were all dressed in our Sunday clothes. Mr. and Mrs. Mares were expecting us and they also were dressed in their best clothes. We entered through the front door. The front door was only used for special occasions. Rose and I left the living room and went into the kitchen to await the outcome. From the kitchen we could hear the conversation in the living room. It was my Uncle Frank who spoke up first. He was very formal and respectful when he asked my future in-laws for their blessing on our union. Rose's dad gave his blessing and Rose and I joined our parents in the living room for coffee and cake. We were married on Thanksgiving Day, November 30, 1939[9], two years from the Thanksgiving Day that we first met. Our first child, Linda, was born on October 7, 1940.

---

7. Dawson, New Mexico, was another coal camp in the area.

8. Rose's parents were Francisco (Frank) and Luisa Tafoya Mares.

9. President Franklin D. Roosevelt had declared November 23 as the official Thanksgiving Day, but many states observed Thanksgiving on November 30. That year, 1939, was known as the year with two Thanksgivings.

Figure 1-4: Francisco (Frank) Mares (July 24, 1884 - May 23, 1959)

Figure 1-5: Luisa Tafoya Mares (January 29, 1884 - January 20, 1966)

That Thanksgiving Day of 1937 turned out to be a lucky day for my buddy John Trujillo as well. He and Pauline Quintana also started dating and were then married in 1940, just a few months after Rose and I were married. This friendship is still strong today. John lost Pauline to cancer in 1994, and I lost Rose to cancer in 2005. John and I stay in touch by phone.

Figure 1-6: Mr. and Mrs. Vincent Silva, November 30, 1939, Ratón, NM

After we married, we lived in Ratón with Rose's parents. I continued to work in the mines in Brilliant, and Rose continued to work as the candy girl at J.J. Newberry's, the local five-and-dime store. On one occasion, my father brought Rose to the mine to pick me up after work. My father asked Rose if she could recognize me from the group of men leaving the mine entrance. She wasn't able to distinguish me from the other miners. We all looked the same – covered with black coal dust from head to toe. It did not take my new wife long to convince me that going down into the depths of the earth to dig coal out of the ground was not the best way for me to make a living.

By the time Linda was born, I had quit the mine and was working for the County of Colfax. This job was a political position. As long as the Democrats were in office the job was mine. After the Republicans won the next election, I was out of work. I had given up my coal-mining job. It was still the Depression years and I was a Democrat. I had two options: I could live off my wife and her family, or I could enlist in the New Mexico National Guard.

Enlisting in the National Guard

In March 1941, against my young wife's wishes, I joined the New Mexico National Guard. As a new recruit in the National Guard, I was sent to Fort Bliss, Texas, where I was assigned to the 200th Coast Artillery (AA). This is when I became number 38011906. For six months we underwent intensive anti-aircraft training. During this time I had one visit from Rose. She took the bus from Ratón to El Paso, Texas. I met her at the bus station in El Paso. The army provided temporary housing for visiting family. Rose and I had one week together before she had to go back home to Linda. Our daughter was in Ratón with Rose's mom and dad. Before getting on the bus, she kissed me goodbye, and placed her rosary in my hand. Neither Rose nor I knew on that day what hardships we had in front of us.

After six months of training, my unit, the 200th Coast Artillery (AA), competed with the regular army at Randolph Field.[10] Had we known at the time that the winner of this competition would be sent to the Philippine Islands, we may not have been so anxious to do our best.

Official citation: United States Army,

17 August 1941

"The 200th is hereby named the best anti-aircraft Regiment (regular or other), now available to the United States armed forces for use in an area of critical military importance."

In August 1941, as the winners of this competition, the 200th CA (AA) was sent to Fort Mason in San Francisco, California. While in Fort Mason we received our new orders. We were to be transported by ship to the Philippine Islands.

---

10. Randolph Air Force Base, Texas, about 15 miles northeast of San Antonio.

SGT Vincent Silva

This was my first trip to San Francisco and the Pacific Coast. I had no idea then that this would become my home after the war. To this small town boy, the city was overwhelming. I remember walking up Market Street with my good friend, Bob Pintarelli from Iron Mountain, Michigan, also a small town. We did not leave that one street for fear we would get lost.

Figure 1-7: Vincent Silva and Robert Pintarelli, circa 1941

From Fort Mason, we were ferried to Fort McDowell on Angel Island, a small island in the middle of the San Francisco Bay. Angel Island has 180-degree views of the Golden Gate Bridge, the San Francisco-Oakland Bay Bridge, San Francisco, and the other cities surrounding the San Francisco Bay. The number of GIs on Angel Island was so large that the mess hall had to serve breakfast three times a day, lunch three times a day, and supper three times a day. It was so crowded on the Island that we barely had space to set up a pup tent to sleep in. After three days we returned to San Francisco where we, the 200th Coast Artillery (AA), boarded the USS *President Coolidge*. The USS *President Coolidge* in its prior life had been a luxury liner. Our government had converted it into a troop transport ship in preparation for war.

We left San Francisco Bay on September 9, 1941, on our way to Honolulu, Hawaii, and then on to Manila Bay in the Philippine Islands. I stood on the deck of the USS *President Coolidge* as it sailed under the Golden Gate Bridge not knowing when I would return to my homeland.

It took four days to reach the island of Oahu. The weather was good and the sailing smooth. We stopped at Pearl Harbor for the better part of one day. While in Pearl Harbor, we were allowed to leave the ship and travel into

Honolulu. The city was very similar to what I had just left in San Francisco. I was surprised at the number of men and women I saw in military uniform. We had just enough time to have lunch and return to our ship.

In the late afternoon, we left Pearl Harbor. The ship made a brief stop at Midway Island before taking us to our destination, Manila, the capital of the Philippine Islands. After we left Midway and were back on the open sea, we were given new orders, "The smoking lamp is out." We were on blackout. No smoking was allowed. The ship was now traveling in darkness.

On September 16, 1941, I along with 1,800 soldiers from the 200th CA (AA) arrived in Manila. This was just eighty-three days before what President Franklin D. Roosevelt would call "a date which will live in infamy."

Chapter 2: World War II

Arrival in Manila

We unloaded our trucks, guns, and other equipment at the Port of Manila. The city of Manila was full of activity. It seemed that every other person I saw was in military uniform – men and women, American and Filipino.

The people of Manila were happy to see the addition of American troops entering their city. It gave them a sense of security. The Japanese will never attack the Philippine Islands with the strength and protection of the U.S. military. Or so they thought.

After unloading our equipment from the USS *President Coolidge*, we were immediately escorted to Fort Stotsenberg in northern Luzon[1], and the USS *President Coolidge*, the ship that had taken me from San Francisco to Manila, was sent on to Australia where (I learned after the war) it was hit by a mine and sank[2].

Figure 2-1: The USS *President Coolidge*

The road out of Manila was full of GIs. Some were walking, some were in jeeps, and some were in trucks like we were. For most of the sixty or more dusty miles, we were traveling on no more than a one-lane dirt road. We drove past Filipino farmers hard at work in the rice fields, their straw hats protecting

---

1. Luzon is the largest of the Philippine Islands.

2. On October 26, 1942, the USS *President Coolidge* loaded with troops, weapons, vehicles, and army supplies, hit two "friendly" mines just a few miles from its destination, Luganville harbor on the Pacific island of Espíritu Santo in Vanuatu. Nearly all of the 5,000 officers and men on board were saved.

them from the hot and humid tropical sun. This was my first day traveling through the jungles of the Philippine Islands. I remember my comrades and I laughing at the monkeys swinging from tree to tree.

Fort Stotsenberg was situated next to Clark Field. This was to be our home for the next three months. Because we were anti-aircraft gunners, it was the ideal post for us. Our orders were to protect Clark Field from enemy attack.

The Attack on Clark Field

On Monday, December 8, 1941 (which was also, because of the international date line, Sunday, December 7, 1941, in Pearl Harbor), the Imperial Army of Japan attacked Clark Field.

It was a warm tropical day, unlike the cold and snowy December days that I remembered from living in northeastern New Mexico. I had been reading *Life Magazine* and I heard my buddy Bob Pintarelli say, "Look, Vince, we're getting in some new planes. The Japs will never attack us now." As I looked up, I could hear the planes and see them off at a distance. Then Lieutenant Richards started to yell, "Everyone to his gun position! Those are Jap planes coming in!" I jumped up from my pup tent, threw down the magazine, and ran to my position. By the time I got to my gun and jumped up on the seat where I could reach the controls, the bombs had started falling on planes and hangars at Clark Field.

The bombing started at about noon, and by 1:00 P.M. I had gotten my first kill. I was now a seasoned veteran. We were shooting at airplanes. I'm not sure I could have shot another man. On that day as I was fighting the enemy, I told myself, "I will not die here. I am going to go back to my wife and daughter." Over the next four years, these thoughts kept me alive and helped me survive as a prisoner of the Japanese.

The Japanese destroyed most of Clark Field and then went on to bomb Nichols Field near the city of Manila. This attack on the first day of the war left the Philippine Islands with nothing more than a skeletal air force to protect it. That same day after the bombing was over, I returned to my pup tent and found both the tent and the *Life Magazine* full of bullet holes.

Our government knew that eventually we were going to fight the Japanese. We had cut off their supply of oil and it was only a matter of time before they would be forced to respond. This was only the beginning of the military build up of the Philippines. The U.S. government thought we had another year to prepare. The Japanese didn't allow for that. They hit us before we were ready. It is said that Admiral Isoroku Yamamoto of Japan had predicted on that day,

> *"We have awakened a sleeping giant and have instilled in him a terrible resolve."*

The 515th CA (AA)

After the attack, our officers decided to split the 200th CA (AA) into two anti-aircraft regiments. So, the 515th CA (AA) was formed. The 200th CA (AA) remained at Fort Stotsenberg to protect Clark Field. Those of us who were assigned to the 515th CA (AA) left Fort Stotsenberg in the early hours of December 9. We drove back to Manila where, at Wall City, we picked up new supplies and equipment. We stayed in Wall City, an old Spanish prison camp, for two days. From there we were sent to a baseball field in Manila called Nichols Field next to the airbase also named Nichols Field. We set up our guns on the baseball field in preparation for any further attacks on Nichols Field airbase. We camped under the bleachers. We spent the first night cleaning our 37-millimeter anti-aircraft guns. We were now on a playing field ready for a different kind of "game."

While in Manila, we were under Japanese air attack almost daily. We stayed there until December 24. By that time the Japanese had just about knocked out all military targets in and around the city. We left Manila on Christmas Eve. Battery G, in which I belonged, was then sent to protect the bridge at Calumpit, about twenty miles outside of Manila. The bridge at Calumpit was very important because it was the only route the American troops had out of Manila. We fought all Christmas Day and were successful in keeping the Japanese planes from blowing up the bridge. If the Japanese had blown up that bridge, our vehicles, our supplies, and all our troops would have been unable to cross the river. Thousands of GIs would have been trapped on the other side. My Christmas dinner was a can of pork and beans. My prayer that night was to thank God for a successful day. The only Christmas wish I had that day was to be home with my family. Little did I know that this was to be my Christmas wish for the next four years.

The evacuation of Manila was completed and in late December 1941, the city of Manila was declared an open city. The U.S. government no longer occupied and protected the citizens of Manila from the Japanese. After the successful evacuation of our troops from Manila, our army engineers destroyed the bridge at Calumpit. We were then sent to the Bataan Peninsula where we met up with the 200th CA (AA). I spent the next three and half months on Bataan fighting the Japanese.

Figure 2-2: Coat of Arms of the 200th CA (AA) and the 515th CA (AA)

Presidential Unit Citations

For our performance during this action, we received a Presidential unit citation which reads as follows:

> *The 515th Coast Artillery anti-aircraft, United States Army Forces in the Far East, is cited for outstanding performance of duty in action. Constituted initially as a provisional unit on December 8, 1941, when hostilities began it affected its organization, obtained its material from depot stocks, and was in position to fire by daylight of December 9, 1941. During the period from December 9, 1941, to December 26, 1941, this regiment defended initially Nichols Field and portions of the city of Manila against heavy aerial attacks, materially reducing the effectiveness of the hostile bombardment. After the evacuation of Manila, this regiment contributed in large measure to the successful execution of the difficult movement that made possible the defense of Bataan.*

The regiment received a second citation, which reads as follows:

> *The 200th Coast Artillery, Anti-Aircraft and the 515th Coast Artillery Anti-Aircraft, United States Army Forces in the Far East, are cited for outstanding performance of duty in action. From January 7 to March 8, 1942, these regiments were constantly in action on the Bataan Peninsula, covering aircraft, artillery, and rear installations. Under constant attack by an enemy enjoying unopposed superiority in the air, these regiments, despite heavy losses of men and material, maintained a magnificent defense through outstanding technical ability and courage and devotion to duty, contributing in large measure to the successful defense of the Bataan Peninsula.*

We Were Expendable

The drive into Bataan was completed and gun sites were assigned to our batteries. We set up our guns at Cabcaben Airfield and from there we helped to protect the peninsula of Bataan from Japanese aircraft. Not only were we responsible for shooting down the enemies' aircraft, but we also had to watch for snipers.

During this time the rumors we heard were that a large convoy of men and supplies from the U.S. was on its way and would soon reach us. Soldiers would stand guard at Mariveles watching for the convoy that never arrived. After the war, we discovered the truth. Our government had decided to send all of its military forces to fight the war in Europe. The men of the Pacific Theater were expendable. We were expected to fight with what we had for as long as we could. Our job was to keep the Japanese fighting in the Philippines and prevent them from reaching and taking Australia. The Japanese never reached Australia.

Figure 2-3: Vince with a 37-Millimeter Anti-Aircraft Gun, Santa Fé, NM 2006

Our guns, the 37-millimeters, were for training purposes only. They had a foot-operated trigger and hand-operated wheel to turn the barrel. They were WW I vintage and the ammunition we were given was either a dud or was corroded. We were supposed to get 40-millimeter guns with the next convoy. We did what we could with what we had. I was one of a two-man crew on a

37-millimeter anti-aircraft gun. My partner during this time was Fausto Noche of Lordsburg, New Mexico. The 37-millimeter had a limited range of 20,000 feet. The Japanese pilots soon learned that to avoid a hit from our guns, they had only to fly a few hundred yards above our range. Even with this disadvantage, my partner and I got credit for shooting down seven planes. Shooting at a plane that is dropping bombs on you is one thing. I'm grateful I never had to shoot face-to-face at another human.

Throughout the next three months, the Japanese launched heavy and continual attacks on the Bataan Peninsula. Every time they tried to advance, we were able to stop them with a heavy barrage of artillery fire. They suffered heavy losses and were forced to withdraw.

Gen. Douglas MacArthur left the Philippine Islands on March 11, 1942, for Australia under direct orders from Washington. Rear Admiral Francis W. Rockwell, Lt. Gen. Richard K. Sutherland (1893-1966), and about twenty other officers left for Australia with Gen. MacArthur. The Philippine Islands were now under the direct orders of Maj. Gen. Edward P. King (1884-1958) and Gen. Jonathan Wainwright (1883-1953).

In April 1942, we saw the heaviest fighting. By this time we were completely out of supplies. We had no food, no ammunition, no replacements, and no hope that any of what we needed was on its way. We had nothing left to stop the Japanese from advancing. Gen. King decided to try and save as many of our soldiers as possible. He knew that to resist would be suicidal. Early in the morning of April 9, 1942, we were ordered to destroy our 37-millimeter anti-aircraft guns and to go to the front lines with our rifles. That made us infantrymen.

Chapter 3: The Surrender of Bataan

April 9, 1942

On April 9, 1942, the American officer in charge of Bataan, Maj. Gen. Edward P. King, went forward under a white flag and surrendered Bataan to our enemy. When the Japanese discovered that he was not Gen. Jonathan Wainwright and he was not surrendering all of the Philippine Islands, they would not accept his surrender. Gen. King had to explain that he was only in charge of the troops at Bataan and therefore could only surrender those troops at Bataan. The Japanese finally accepted his surrender and on April 10, 1942, the Japanese under the command of Gen. Masaharu Homma took over 70,000 American and Filipino service men and women prisoners. The 200th CA (AA) represented 1,780 of those captured. Of the 1,800 who arrived in the Philippines with me, we had lost only twenty of our men. By the end of World War II, our numbers were reduced to less than 900.

After the surrender, the Japanese searched all the prisoners and seized their belongings. Those with Japanese money or tokens were beheaded, stabbed with bayonets, or shot to death. I saw, almost directly in front of me, a captain shot in the head by a Japanese guard with a pistol the guard had found in the captain's backpack. When it was my turn to be searched, the Japanese guard found the rosary that Rose had given to me the last time we were together almost one year before. He placed his hands together as if in prayer and bowed his head. I nodded yes to him, and he gave the rosary back to me and went on to search the next POW. That same rosary, the one my wife had given to me back in El Paso, Texas, was with me three and half years later when I was liberated from the Japanese.

The Japanese sat us in rows at Cabcaben Airfield. Then they brought in their big guns and placed them behind us and started to shell Corregidor. From Cabcaben we could see Corregidor and the men on Corregidor could see us. The Japanese knew that Corregidor would not fire back at their fellow American soldiers.

While being used as human shields, we could see the PT boats[1] fighting the Zeroes (Japanese fighter planes). No one dared to show any sign of joy or excitement when one of the Zeros was shot down, but we all knew which side we were silently cheering for.

Gen. Wainwright was forced to surrender Corregidor and the remaining American troops on May 6, 1942. By that time, the Bataan Death March had been completed.

I was in one of the first groups to be removed from Cabcaben Airfield. We had no idea at that time where we were going or what hardships we were to face. What we did know was that our lives were now in the hands of the Japanese.

---

1. PT boats were small, wooden crafts that carried enough firepower to sink a battleship, were faster than anything on the water, and could sneak right up to shore to perform reconnaissance or drop off troops.

Chapter 4: The Bataan Death March

My 24th Birthday

We began the March in groups of 500 to 1,000 men. We were given no water nor food. We walked until dark, then we were all packed into a barbed wire enclosure with no room to move. The next day began in the stench and filth of that enclosure. We were all hungry, thirsty, and sick. The Japanese brought in one spigot for the thousands of men needing water. It was impossible for everyone to drink from this one spigot. Being thirsty and without water is worse than hunger. Your tongue swells and your lips crack.

If there was any pushing or arguing in the line, the guards beat us. One of the men in line was not pushing nor arguing, but he got in the way of a guard and the Japanese guard stuck about three inches of his bayonet into the man's rump. This was a time of strong will. Those that couldn't go on died where they fell, or were shot by the guards, or stabbed with bayonets and left to die.

As we started out on the second day of the Death March, the rumors started flying. The Filipinos have large pots of steaming rice at the next stop and there are artesian wells to drink from. We will get plenty of clear, cool water, all we want. The older and more experienced officers kept the rumors going, and of course, this put a little spring to our walking and lifted our spirits. Just think — bowls of steaming rice and plenty of fresh water to drink.

I marked my 24th birthday on April 12, 1942. This was three days into the Bataan Death March. I was thankful to still be alive.

Deplorable Conditions

A lot of the experiences that we went through are fading from my memory. This happened so many, many years ago. I do remember at one small village where we had stopped, we were lined up on one side of the road. Across from us we could see an artesian well bubbling up clear, sweet, fresh water from the earth. We, of course, expected to be able to drink and fill our canteens. After awhile, one of the men broke and ran for the well. He was immediately attacked by the guards, knocked to the ground and stabbed with bayonets. It is such a helpless feeling to watch a man dying in the dust, knowing you can do nothing to help him.

The water we did get was from the caribou wallows, puddles of water that the caribou used to wallow in, or from a dirty roadside stream. Of course, the water was contaminated and many of the men became sick with dysentery from drinking this water. If you became sick and could not continue, you were shot or beheaded. It is also true that some of our soldiers were buried while still alive.

The guards lined us up at daylight, put us into columns, and kept us standing at attention until the sun was high above. The tropical sun of the Philippines is hot and the climate humid. Then they started us off at double-time, and when the line was stretched out, they would bring us back together and have us stand again in the hot sun. This was our routine for most of the Death March. When sick and exhausted men fell out of line, no one was allowed to help. The bodies of the dead lay along the road, flattened by Japanese trucks.

Figure 4-1: The Bataan Death March

We sometimes found rice balls and cups with water on the side of the road left for us by the Filipino citizens. If a guard discovered a citizen leaving food or water for the POWs, that Filipino citizen would be shot or beheaded.

Every night was the same. We were herded into barbed wire enclosures with no food, no water, and no room to move. Because so many of our men were sick with malaria and dysentery and no place to move inside the enclosure, it got pretty bad and stinky by the morning.

The length of the Bataan Death March was about seventy miles. Not really that far, but the conditions under which we were forced to march – no water, no food, the hot tropical sun – made the March deadly. American GIs march that far all the time but with a cook that prepares all the meals, with plenty of fresh water, with sleeping bags and pup tents. It is estimated that over 5,000 POWs lost their lives along those seventy miles.

Figure 4-2: Along the March (National Archives photo)

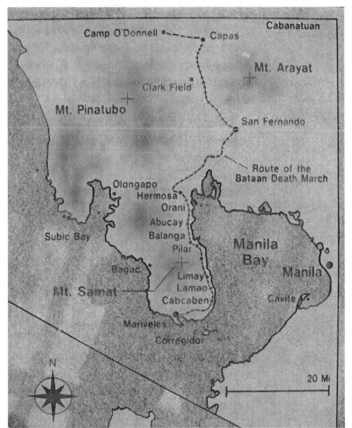

Figure 4-3: Route of the Bataan Death March (Photo from Bataan Memorial Park, Albuquerque, NM)

Chapter 5: Camp O'Donnell

"And As Such You Shall be Treated"

The Bataan Death March ended with our arrival at Camp O'Donnell on Luzon. Camp O'Donnell had been a Filipino military camp. It was now being used by the Japanese as a prisoner of war camp. When we first arrived at the camp, we were told to sit on the ground and wait. The camp commander, Gen. Tomoyuki Yamashita (1885-1946)[1], wanted to speak to us. Gen. Masaharu Homma (1887-1946)[2] had been relieved of his command in the Philippines because he had failed to conquer the natives and the Americans fighting there. Japan's Prime Minister Tojo Hideki ordered Gen. Yamashita from Malaya to take over the Philippine Islands from Gen. Homma and to beat the Allies into submission. The troops on Corregidor[3] were still fighting the Japanese with the scant supplies that they had left. Gen. Yamashita was known as the Tiger of Malaysia, the "cruelest, meanest man alive." The General was having lunch, so we waited. After an hour or more, Gen. Yamashita emerged to give his speech. He proceeded to lay down the law. "Do this and you will be shot, don't do that and you will be shot." Even though he had studied in the United States, he spoke to us through an interpreter. It was beneath him to speak to us in our language. The one thing that stands out in my mind about that speech is when he said:

> *"America and Japan have always been enemies, and we shall always be enemies, and now you are prisoners of war and as such you shall be treated."*

Those words are burned into my mind.

---

1. Gen. Yamashita was found guilty of war crimes and hanged February 23, 1946.

2. After the surrender of the Japanese, Homma was convicted by a U.S. military commission in the Philippines of war crimes, including the atrocities of the Death March out of Bataan, and the atrocities at camps O'Donnell and Cabanatuan that followed, and executed by firing squad on April 3, 1946, outside Manila.

3. Corregidor was not surrendered until May 6, 1942.

Conditions at the Camp

We opened up Camp O'Donnell and did what we could to make it livable. But living conditions were bad there. We had very little food and no medical supplies. Many men crawled into Camp after the Death March, only to die a day or two later. Those of us who were able buried our comrades. During the days after the March, we buried anywhere from one hundred to two hundred men every day. At this rate it was hard not to think ... *When will it be my turn?* The men were dying of disease and starvation. It was tragic that these men had survived the Death March, only to die in the Camp. It did not take us long to give Camp O'Donnell the nickname "Camp O'Death." During this time, I buried two of my cousins – Amadeo Archuleta and Benito Paiz – and my wife's cousin, John Romero. All three had been members of the 200th CA (AA). Men were dying by the thousands with no relief in sight. We lost a lot of good men and a lot of them were from New Mexico.

Figure 5-1: "Rules and Regulations," drawing by Ben Steele, Bataan Survivor

We stayed at Camp O'Donnell for about two months. It is estimated that over 2,000 American soldiers lost their lives during that time. At the end of those two months, we were ordered to break camp and prepare to move. That is when we were sent to Camp Cabanatuan.

Fence Posts

We walked the three miles to Capas, and there we were packed like sardines into boxcars. The train ride lasted about six or seven hours in unbearable heat. It felt as if we were being cooked alive in hot ovens. The air was so humid that we could hardly breathe. We were packed together so tightly that the men who died were unable to fall to the floor of the boxcars.

We left the train in the town of Cabanatuan and walked to the POW camp, about four miles outside of town. We were to discover at this POW camp what had happened to the GIs fighting on the island of Corregidor. Gen. Wainwright had direct orders from Washington and Gen. MacArthur to fight the Japanese to the last man. On May 6, 1942, almost one month after the surrender of Bataan, Gen. Wainwright went against orders and surrendered Corregidor. His men had nothing with which to continue fighting the Japanese. The men on Corregidor were taken to the POW camp at Cabanatuan by truck and by train. Only the men surrendered on Bataan experienced the Death March.

As we walked up to Camp Cabanatuan, one memory stands out in my mind. I will never forget the fence posts. On each post was a human head. That was a reminder to every prisoner of what would happen if we tried to escape. I realized then that the only escape from this hell-hole was death.

SGT Vincent Silva

Chapter 6: Camp Cabanatuan

Life In Cabanatuan

Soon after our arrival at Camp Cabanatuan, I was surprised by a visit from a cousin, Valentín Shipley. He had been a medical corpsmen on the Island of Corregidor before the surrender. When he discovered that the POWs from Bataan were arriving in Cabanatuan, he went searching for me. I was suffering with dry beriberi when he found me. Because he was a medic, he had access to the only treatment available in camp, quinine pills. He brought me enough quinine to heal me from the constant disabling pain in my legs and feet. He stayed with me and nursed me back to health. He was also with me when I became infected with malaria. My cousin Val Shipley and his stash of quinine saved my life twice during the first few months that I was in Camp Cabanatuan. It was discovered after the war that the Japs had more then enough quinine and other medicines in their stockrooms to save thousands of American and Filipino lives. These stockrooms also contained food and Red Cross packages. None of it was given out to our sick and dying men.

My cousin Val was one of the first to be taken from Cabanatuan on a hell ship to Japan. He spent most of the war as a slave working in Japanese factories. We reunited in Manila after the war ended. He stayed in the military and retired after twenty years.

After our arrival at Camp Cabanatuan, things seemed to get a little better. Our camp doctors received medical supplies from some of the concerned citizens of Manila. The death rate decreased and we were able to control the dysentery, malaria, and beriberi that had taken so many lives.

The Japanese had commandeered about ten square miles of land next to the camp. One of our duties was to clear a large section of this land. This was to be used for a vegetable farm. About 1,500 POWs including myself were used as farm laborers.

Although I had worked in the vegetable garden on our family ranch when I was young, working the farm for the Japanese was far more difficult. We didn't have any regular farming tools like hoes and shovels, but instead we used small scoops and our bare hands to plant seeds and weed, digging and sowing on our hands and knees. The Japanese didn't even allow us to wear shoes. They didn't want us to trample the crops.

While clearing the land, we were always on the lookout for a mature cobra or even better, its nest where we would rob it of its eggs. Dead snakes and cobra eggs were brought into camp where they would make a tasty supplement to our scant evening meal. Iguana tail was also a tasty treat. And being Americans, we missed our coffee. But the Japanese didn't provide the prisoners with coffee, so we improvised by taking burnt rice and boiling it for brown water. It wasn't exactly coffee, but dead snakes and cobra eggs weren't home-cooked meals either.

Work Details

While we were in Cabanatuan, many work details were made up and sent to different parts of the countryside. Some went to Cavite, a submarine base, or to the island of Mindanao, or to Manila. Every few weeks we would say goodbye to friends who were being sent out on these details. Sadly, some of these men were never seen again.

When our men did return from the work details, they brought back tales of horrible atrocities. They had endured starvation, torture, and of course there were always stories of the murders by the Japanese guards.

We found that the cruelest of the Japanese guards were the ones that had been born or educated in the United States. They had gone to Japan to help in the war effort. It seemed that they had to prove to their commanders that they were true Japanese and not Americans.

Other small work details would leave camp in the morning and return that night with food rations or firewood and always with rumors. The Marines were landing on some of the southern islands. The rumors were good for our morale. They kept our hopes up, and for some of the men these rumors saved their lives. For me, the memory of a loving wife and my baby girl did more to keep me alive than all the rumors.

Our days were filled with the different jobs in and around the camp. There was the farm to work, the honey bucket detail, and we always had burial detail. The camp itself needed to be maintained and kept clean.

Because human waste from the honey buckets was used to fertilize the vegetables, we had to boil them and boil them hard before they were consumed. Even so, many of us still came down with dysentery. The death rate at Cabanatuan was not as bad as it had been in Camp O'Donnell. We still lost many of our men to disease and many more to the brutality of the Japanese guards.

More Brutality

The Japanese guards found great pleasure in torturing our men. One execution in particular stands out in my mind. A POW was caught trading with a guard. The guard, to protect himself, accused this POW of trying to escape. The Japs took the American, sat him on the ground with his hands tied behind him and around a fence post. He was left there for two days. The rest of the Americans in camp knew that if one of us went to give him aid or comfort, that POW would be shot, or worse yet, be placed in the same torture. Each time a Jap guard passed this POW during the two days he was tied to the fence post, the guard would kick him. At the end of the two days they marched him out into the field, in plain view of the camp, so we could all watch. There they had him kneel with his hands still tied behind him. The guard that had wrongly accused him of trying to escape took his gun and shot the POW in the head. This American soldier's name was Juan Trujillo. He was from Springer, New Mexico, and he was a friend of mine.

The Japanese had executed many of our men, claiming that they were caught trying to escape. Towards the end of 1942, they came up with a brilliant idea. They divided us into groups of ten. If one of the ten tried to escape, the other nine men would be executed. After that, we made sure that there were no further attempts to escape.

Life varied at Cabanatuan depending on the guards and the camp commander. Some were almost human and during that time we had a little peace in the camp. It was in the fall of 1942 that the priests in the camp convinced the commander to allow them to hold Mass on Sundays. Many of the POWs attended Mass, regardless of their religious background. From time to time we would even have some of the guards join us at Sunday Mass.

Passing Time

On special occasions, we were allowed to watch movies, and some Filipinos from Manila gave us musical instruments. We constructed a stage where our talented POWs presented plays for us. One of the performers was a piano player named Melody. After the war, I saw him in San Francisco performing with a western singer named Rusty Draper. I was able to talk to Melody for a short time after the show, and Rusty Draper gave me an autograph.

We had time in the evenings during the long Philippine twilight to think of home and share stories of our lives before the war. It seemed that no matter what the subject, we always ended up talking about food. We all had our favorite dishes and we enjoyed telling our friends about them and hearing them tell their stories. We talked incessantly about our families, about getting home, and how great it would be to once again live in peace.

Rumors and Stories

The rumors at Cabanatuan were flying constantly. With each returning detail we were told a new story. We heard that the largest convoy ever assembled in the history of the world had left the U.S. and was heading for the Philippines to liberate us. We also heard that Japanese forces had invaded the west coast of the United States. Most stories we took for what they were, just rumors. Once in awhile a true story would come into camp.

Boy Hero

One returning detail told us a story concerning a very brave twelve-year-old Filipino schoolboy. He had been with the guerrillas, fighting in the jungles. He would go into surrounding towns and villages and gather information and supplies vital to the guerrillas. This information was used to plan when to attack, how to attack, and where the most important targets were located. In this way the guerrillas were able to destroy munitions dumps, motor pools, and blow up bridges.

The Japs finally found out about the boy and captured him. They beat him mercilessly trying to get him to reveal the hiding place of the guerillas, but the boy stubbornly refused to say anything. Finally, after a few days of interrogation and torture, the boy admitted that he knew where the guerrillas were hiding. He told them that he couldn't tell them where but he could show them the hiding place. The Japanese sent the young boy out in a truck loaded with Jap soldiers to find the guerilla camp. In the front sat the driver, the boy, and one Japanese officer. The boy then led them to a winding road high in the mountains with a deep canyon on one side. As they were driving along, the boy grabbed the steering wheel and turned the truck, crashing it down the canyon. The boy was killed along with all the Japs in that truck. This story proved to be true, but the name of the boy escapes me.

The Hell Ships

On many occasions our American POWs would be sent by ship to work as slaves in Japan. Some of these ships never made it. They were torpedoed by our own submarines. At least that was the report we received in Cabanatuan. The one I remember most vividly is the ship that was carrying my good friend Robert Pintarelli. We had been together since Fort Bliss, Texas. The ship that Bob was on was hit by an American torpedo and sank. It sank near land and some of the POWs, including Bob, were able to swim back to shore only to be captured again by the Japanese. Once more they were sent on their way to Japan. Their next ship, the *Arisan Maru*[1], was also torpedoed by our subs, but this time no one survived.

In the spring of 1944, the American officers at Cabanatuan were ordered to pick out 150 men for a work detail. I was picked for this detail. We left Cabanatuan without knowing what our destination was. I found myself back at Fort Stotsenberg. Our work there was to maintain the airstrip at Clark Field now under the control of the Japanese.

Clark Field was being used to train Japanese recruits to be pilots. Several times while working on the airfield, we would witness planes crashing into each other in the air. This would result in the loss of two Japanese planes and two Japanese pilots. We, on the ground, could only cheer inwardly and smile to each other.

After several months at Clark Field, the Japanese commander sent word to our camp commander to raise a detail of 150 men. I was selected for that detail and we were to leave in three days. When the time came we were loaded onto trucks. Our destination was Manila where we were to be loaded onto a ship for Japan.

---

1. The *Arisan Maru* was torpedoed and sank on October 24, 1944.

Chapter 7: The *Noto Maru*

Packed Like Sardines

In Manila, we were held at Bilibid Prison for six days as preparations were made for our departure to Japan. We spent the days in Bilibid walking around the courtyard, waiting in the chow line, or reminiscing with buddies about our home life. We were always hungry, so our conversations would invariably end up around food. We could vividly remember the home-cooked meals, the Thanksgiving dinners, the kitchen table loaded with good things to eat. At night I would dream of food only to wake the next morning with my stomach rumbling. My repeating dream was of a big breakfast of hot cakes, eggs, and bacon. Just as I was about to take the first bite … I would wake up.

On the sixth day, we were marched through the streets of Manila. We were on our way to the pier and the *Noto Maru*, the ship that would transport us to Japan. As we marched through the city, the wonderful citizens of Manila lined the streets to throw rice cakes and coconut candy and hold up two fingers, giving us the "V" for victory sign. There was always the chance that, if seen by a Japanese guard, they would be beaten or killed. I have great respect for the Filipino people and what they endured during the occupation of the Philippine Islands by the Japanese.

There was some evidence of war in Manila, but it wasn't major because it had been declared an open city on December 24, 1941. The "Pearl of the Orient" was no longer the beautiful and lively city of pre-war days. When we arrived at the port area, I looked back and wondered, *Will I ever see Manila again?*

After boarding the *Noto Maru*, we were sent to the bottom of the hold. We were ordered to sit and the next man would sit between the legs of the man behind him until the hold was full. A total of 1,162 men were packed like sardines in the hold of the *Noto Maru*. We boarded the ship on August 13, 1944, and sailed out of Manila Harbor two days later.

The Japanese guards warned us that there would be no smoking in the hold. If anyone was caught smoking, the guards would turn their machine guns on all of us. The American senior officer, Capt. George Sense, told us that if anyone lit a cigarette, he would personally work him over with a bar of soap in a sock.

As we slowly steamed toward Formosa, the days were hot, stuffy, and very long. Our daily meal during this transport consisted of one ball of rice and a half cup of water. We had been given a few honey buckets to relieve ourselves. Each morning the buckets would be pulled out of the hold by some of our men. It was a dirty job, but the ones that really had it bad were the men seated directly under the hold opening. The buckets were always overflowing and the unfortunate men directly under the ascending buckets would get an unwelcomed shower of human waste.

Figure 7-1: The *Noto Maru* "Hell Ship"

After several days in that sweltering hold, the Japanese allowed us to go on deck in groups of forty to fifty men where we received a shower of sea water from their hoses. It was refreshing and cool on our sweaty, dirty clothes and bodies.

We arrived in Takao, Formosa, after eleven or twelve days at sea. We were put ashore and placed in an old warehouse. There we could walk around and stretch. It felt good to stretch after the cramped position we were forced to live in for so many days. We were given hot, steaming bowls of barley that night and again the next morning. The supply lines to Japan were being lost to the approaching Allied forces. The food and rice that did come through was sent to the fighting troops at the front lines. That left only barley for the civilians and the prisoners. That day we were again packed in the hold of the *Noto Maru* and steamed out of the harbor to continue our journey to Japan.

Soon after we left Formosa, American submarines attacked the convoy we were in. We could hear the torpedoes as they shot past us and we could feel a lot of thuds which were depth charges exploding beneath us. We heard and felt one tremendous explosion and saw a big glare in the sky. We all figured that one of our torpedoes had hit a Japanese tanker. Everyone inside that hold hollered with both excitement and fear.

There was a lot of speculation among the men as to what they could possibly want us for in Japan. Perhaps we would be working in the coal mines, or in a factory helping with their war effort. And again our thoughts would be on our families, our friends, and always on the home cooked meals. My memories always took me back to the loving wife and baby girl I had waiting for me at home. Every opportunity I had, I brought out the rosary that Rose had given to me and I prayed to go home to my family.

Our pending fate in Japan was very uncertain. In Formosa, we were more or less ignored. Many Americans had already passed through, so we were no longer a curiosity. What could we expect in Japan where the majority of the people had never seen Americans before? Many of the Japanese people had lost loved ones in this war, and we were the Americans that had killed them.

One night the Japanese interpreter told Capt. Sense that we were nearing Japan. The Japanese did not expect to encounter any more American submarines. One of our men overheard this conversation and decided to light up a cigarette. Capt. Sense caught him and worked him over with a bar of soap in a sock, just as he had warned us he would do. The Japanese never knew about the lit cigarette.

Finally we heard a cry from the crew. They had spotted the homeland. We landed in Moji, Japan, on September 6, 1944. It was a coal mining town. We could see the piles of slag that were left over from the coal they shipped to the factories to support the war effort.

Amazingly, we lost only four of our men on this trip. Their bodies had been buried at sea. Were they the lucky ones?

Chapter 8: Life in Japan

Arrival at Moji

We were taken off the *Noto Maru* in the town of Moji. The guards put us into a large warehouse and told us to remove our old clothes. They gave us Japanese military uniforms to wear. This was the first time since the surrender, two and a half years earlier, that I had on clean clothes. Imagine! American soldiers in Japanese military uniforms. We were given a rice ball, a slice of apple, a piece of fish, and fresh water. This food wasn't much, but it was far more than we had eaten in a long time.

On the morning of September 7, 1944, we were separated into several groups. The group I was in was placed aboard a train heading north. During the next three days, the train made several stops. At each stop, the Japanese guards removed large numbers of our men and the train continued north. At the town of Nomachi, I was among a group of one hundred and fifty ordered off the train. We left the train not knowing what our captors had in store for us.

Arrival at Nomachi

The town of Nomachi is a seaport at the northern end of Japan. As we left the train, it seemed that the entire town had come out to look at us. They had never seen Americans. The guards had to keep some of them away from us because they were very angry with the "warmonger Americans."

The guards led us through the town to our new prison camp. Camp Nomachi sat at the outskirts of town. There was a six-foot fence around the barracks and a guard tower with an armed guard next to the fence's large gate. We were taken on a tour of the barracks, a fairly new building. It had a long walkway the length of the building with open rooms on either side. Each room had double bunks against the wall with straw mattresses. The so-called mattresses were harder than a brick. We were each issued two blankets and what they called a pillow made of bamboo. Toward one end of the building was a kitchen and further out was the wash room. The tub in the wash room was a typical Japanese community tub. It was twelve feet by twenty feet, and four feet deep. They kept the water about three feet deep and very hot. There was a fire under the tub and a constant temperature maintained. The Japanese gave us small, waterproof wooden boxes about ten inches by ten inches. We dipped the boxes into the tub of hot water, then lathered up and rinsed off before getting into the community tub. Sitting in the hot water before going to bed was very relaxing.

After our tour of the facility, our camp commander[1] ordered us into the yard where he gave us the rules of the camp. That day we named him the "One Armed Bandit." He had lost his right arm fighting in China. His interpreter was a Japanese citizen who had been raised in Santa Rosa, California. A second interpreter assigned to us was a young American[2], born and raised in Japan. As we stood at attention, the interpreter related what the camp commander was saying.

"Lies, lies, lies! The Japanese soldier is honorable and did not commit atrocities at Bataan!"

He went on to say that the Japanese camp officers ordered their men to protect the prisoners from the "guerillas and bandits" who were roaming the hills and harming the Filipino civilians. The guards would treat us well as long as we did not try to escape. The commander then dismissed us. We went in, washed up, and had our meager dinner. The next day we were introduced to the foundry and our working conditions.

Work at the Foundry

On our first morning the guards awakened us by hollering and stomping their feet. The guards then rushed us out of bed, into our clothes, and out to breakfast. Breakfast was a bowl of barley soup. The guards then walked us back through the town and down to the bay where we boarded a ferry that took us to Takaoka. There we saw the foundry where we were to spend the remainder of the war turning out manganese. The manganese was then shipped to steel mills owned by Mitsubishi for construction of planes to be used by the Japanese kamikaze pilots. As the guard and interpreter took us through the foundry, we saw for the first time the six open-hearth furnaces and the coal piles used to feed the furnaces. Our job was to shovel the coal into the furnaces throughout the day and night. Because the heat was so intense, we were given proper clothing, including large, heavy gloves to work with.

About three weeks after our arrival at Camp Nomachi, 150 British and Irish POWs joined us. These men were captured in Singapore and were brought to Japan soon after their capture. At first we were glad to see them. Unlike the

---

1. Keigi Nagahara. No record of him being captured or tried for war crimes.

2. Probably James T. Boyce, nicknamed "Interpreter."

American POWs, the British had not experienced over two years of prison camp in the Philippines. The British officers kept a pretty tight hold on their men. The enlisted men were expected to salute their officers and they expected us to salute them as well. By that time we were no longer saluting our own officers, and there was no way we were going to salute the British. It became a problem and the Japanese soon found that the Americans and the British would need to be separated. The British worked a twelve-hour shift while the Americans slept, and the Americans worked twelve hours while the British slept. Once a week we changed shifts with the British. On the day of the change we each had to work an 18-hour shift.

Figure 8-1: Prisoners of War at Nomachi; SGT Vincent Silva circled

We soon settled into a daily routine: arise in the morning to a meager breakfast of barley soup, travel with the guards to the foundry, put in our twelve hours of work, travel back with the guards to camp, eat a meager dinner of barley soup, take a hot bath, and sleep. The camp itself was not too bad. It had been built for the Japanese soldiers. The best thing was the hot bath. It seemed to reduce the fatigue and left you relaxed and ready for a much-needed night of sleep.

Our most serious problem was malnutrition. The Japanese gave us just enough food to keep us working. I was always hungry from the day of the surrender until we were liberated. After almost four years of a starvation diet by the Japanese I weighed less than 90 pounds.

I made some good friends among the other POWs. One of the prisoners, Jimmy Jones, was assigned to the shoe shop and he made me a pair of leather boots for the cold winter. He also gave me some left over leather with which I made a pipe holder and a tobacco pouch. Jimmy Jones' dad was the lieutenant governor of New Mexico. Jimmy tried to convince me to return to New Mexico with him after the war and go into politics. My earlier experience with politics in Ratón made it easy for me to turn down that idea.

Two of the men I worked with in the foundry were Dick Joder of Florida, and Will Houser of Wisconsin. The three of us became very good friends. We shared the same bunk and spent many hours talking about our families and our lives before the war.

There were many Japanese women who also worked at the foundry. They were hard, conscientious workers. Some of the women would bring us rice balls and slip them to us when the guards weren't around. The older ones would sit with us during breaks and try to communicate with us. We would carry on a crude form of conversation by means of sign language and gestures. We were helping them with the work, since most of the men were off fighting the war. There were many young women, just girls really, who also worked at the foundry. I guess they were not allowed to talk to us because they stayed away from us at all times.

The winter was very cold with some heavy snowstorms. There was nothing for us to shovel the snow with so we just packed it down when we walked on it. We were issued one jacket and regular hobnailed shoes. There was a small potbelly stove in the middle of the barracks but the heat from it was never enough to warm us. There wasn't much wood to burn. The camp commander, the One Armed Bandit, would on occasion come into the barracks roaring drunk on sake. He would take his saber in his left hand and wave it over his head yelling at us to "Fire the stove up and get it hot." His first sergeant was always with him to interpret for him and to keep him from harming anyone.

During the last few months before the end of the war, the Japanese guards were easily irritated at anything the POWs did. Many of us were beaten for little or no reason. We later discovered that during this time the war was going badly for them. Their troops were being pushed back and all their conquered territories were being taken by the Allies.

The Japanese plan for home defense was to send all the women and children inland where they, along with the POWs, would be executed. By that time the Japanese had over 69,000 POWs in 158 camps throughout the Pacific. When the invasion of Japan began, all able-bodied Japanese men had orders to defend the homeland and Emperor Hirohito (1901-1989) to the last man. To the Japanese, the act of surrender was to lose face. In their eyes, this was worse than death.

"Senso Owari"

Fortunately, the dropping of the atomic bombs on Hiroshima and Nagasaki prevented the Japanese from completing this plan. The lives of the Japanese population were saved, as well as many prisoners and thousands of Allied fighting men.

For me and eight of my fellow prisoners, the timing could not have been better. One evening after a long day of work, about thirty of us were in the fenced enclosure next to the foundry. We were waiting for the ferry to take us back to camp. Next to us was a barge docked on the river. In this barge we could see bags full of vegetables. The guards had left us to check on the ferry and we could see no one onboard the barge. Nine of us climbed the fence and boarded the barge. We stuffed our jackets with soybeans. The guards returned and caught us before we had time to climb back to the other side of the fence. The nine of us were lined up and the guard in charge hit us all in the face. The blow was so hard I thought my jaw was broken. We were taken back to camp and accused of stealing from the Emperor of Japan and trying to escape. Our sentence for this crime was to die by firing squad. The date of our execution was August 15, 1945.

On the morning of August 15, 1945, the Japanese guards stacked their rifles and left. The One Armed Bandit and his first sergeant came into our barracks and ordered us to gather around. He sadly announced to us, *"Senso owari, shigato nai."* ("The war is ended, there will be no more work.") At first we stood in stunned silence, then as if awakened from death, the entire camp was jumping around with joy. We were hugging each other. We were laughing and crying at the same time. I don't believe that any one of us ever thought that we would not win the war. Our only question was: *Would we live long enough to see the end?* We later learned that the actual surrender of the Japanese was on August 9.

Chapter 9: Liberation

Red Cross and Food

After the announcement that the war had ended, it seemed like an eternity before a Red Cross representative arrived at our camp. Actually it was only a few days. When he did arrive we gathered around him. He told us to wait in the camp. Navy planes were coming to pick us up and fly us to Portland, Oregon. From there we would be sent home. He also told us to paint a POW on the roof of our barracks so that Navy pilots could find us and drop food and supplies to us.

It was from this Red Cross representative that we first learned about the dropping of the atomic bomb on Hiroshima and Nagasaki. He tried to explain to us about the terrible destructive power in just one bomb. This information was very frightening to me. I had read before the war about atomic energy and the power behind it. As I listened to the Red Cross representative, I could not help but think that this was the beginning of the end of the world. I was grateful to President Truman for using the bomb to end the war and I still feel that it was the right decision. But the power of it still frightens me.

Soon after we painted the POW on the roof of our barracks, the Navy planes found us. They immediately started to drop parachutes with packages full of food and medical supplies. These were the first medical supplies we had seen in a long, long time. The packages also contained toothbrushes and toothpaste, razors and shaving cream, newspapers and magazines. The things that you take for granted in everyday life, things that we had been denied for so long. It was all such a treat.

The best thing, the most important thing in the parachutes that the Navy planes brought us was the food. We finally had some good American food. Some of the men ate so much that they got sick. Although we were happy with all the supplies the Navy planes were bringing us, we were anxiously waiting for the planes that the Red Cross representative had told us were coming to fly us home.

The Long Wait

During the long days of August waiting for the planes that we were told would be taking us to Portland, we had nothing to do but reminisce. We talked about the atrocities that we had witnessed, the beatings and the beheadings, the murder and the executions for little or no reason. We talked about the brave Filipino men and women who took life threatening chances to help us, leaving balls of rice and cups of water on the side of the road. We shared stories of the horrors that we had experienced.

The American camp commander, Capt. Sense was from Canyon City, Colorado. He was a wise career officer and older than most of us. He would gather us around him and try to explain what we could expect when we got home:

> *"Don't brag about your heroic exploits in this war. Be very careful with your money. You have a large lump sum in back-pay coming to you and you will meet greedy vultures who are waiting to take it from you. Be careful eating the rich food the planes have dropped, your stomachs will need time to get used to it."*

He also told us that our families and our friends back home would never understand the horrors of war that we had experienced. He told us to go home and try to remove the memories of this war from our minds. Capt. Sense told us these things for our own good. It may not have worked out that way. When we got back home we refused to talk at all about our experiences and our loved ones thought they were protecting us by not pressing us for the details. We kept everything inside and the problems kept expanding until in time we exploded with anger. This anger was directed against the very ones who loved us the most and would have done anything to help and protect us.

Train to Freedom

It was mid-September and the planes that were promised had not arrived. The One Armed Bandit and his first sergeant were the only Japanese still with us in Camp Nomachi. Finally, Capt. Sense went to the One Armed Bandit and made it clear to him that he was to provide a train to take all of us to American ships. The next day on September 15, a train was waiting for us. We loaded our gear onto the Japanese passenger train and started out for Tokyo Bay.

The train took us through many cities, towns, and small villages. At many of these towns our train would stop and the people would greet us by bowing very low, to make us understand that they would now be our friends. I could not help but remember the words of Gen. Yamashita on our first day at Camp O'Donnell after the Death March, "*America and Japan have always been enemies, and we shall always be enemies.*"

After two long days in the heat of summer, we entered Tokyo city. No, it was the blackened shell of what was once Tokyo city. For as far as I could see the once grand buildings were gone. In their place I saw nothing but wasteland. The destruction of this war was not only in the gaunt faces and hallowed eyes of the men that sat on the train with me but was also outside the windows of the train. Miles and miles of this once vibrant city were now miles and miles of blackened ruin. The Japanese people that I saw walking on what was left of the streets of Tokyo had the appearance of lost souls. Walking, walking, walking with no place to go.

The train continued to Tokyo Bay. What greeted us as our train turned and we first set sight of Tokyo Bay were the beautiful grand ships of our U.S. Navy. This is where we encountered the first American troops. As I prepared to depart the train, I could tell that something was going on outside. I walked down from the train and in front of me was a Navy hospital ship. The sailors from the ship, in their clean white Navy uniforms, were helping us in our dirty old tattered rags.

Each one of us, as we prepared to board the ship, stood at attention and saluted our flag. Even my fellow ex-POW soldiers who were too weak to walk by themselves to the ship, stood at attention with the help of a sailor and saluted our flag. When it was my turn, tears burned in my eyes as I stood at attention and, with pride in my heart and soul, I saluted Old Glory. The last time I had seen our flag, the symbol of our freedom, was at Cabanatuan. The Japanese guards had thrown it on the ground and were using it to wipe their boots as they entered the huts.

After boarding the hospital ship where we were de-loused and given clean clothes, we threw our old Jap uniforms into the bay. It was great to take a shower and put on new American uniforms.

Did I get my pancakes, eggs, and bacon? You bet I did, and lots of other things, like fresh baked bread and cinnamon rolls. We could order steak three times a day, or anything else that we wanted. This trip to Manila was great. Nothing like the hell-hole on which we had come to Japan. **We were free men again!**

SGT Vincent Silva

Fattening Us Up

When we landed in Manila, we were in such poor physical condition. I weighed just over 100 pounds. Our government did not want our families to see us until we had put on some weight. I spent the next eighteen days in a rest and recuperation camp the Army had set up for us. We were told by the officer in charge, "The mess hall is open twenty-four hours a day with a cook on duty. Anytime you feel like eating, just go to the mess hall and ask." We did a lot of asking. If the cook had it, he would fix it for us. We all gained weight, not just by the day but by the hour. We were also issued two cans of beer and one pack of cigarettes per day. There was a lot of trading and buying going on because some of the men didn't smoke so they would rather have the beer, and surprisingly enough, some of our men didn't care for the beer.

During this time we were free to travel around and visit places of interest. Everywhere we went the Filipino people were happy to see us. The Islands had been liberated in February, seven months before, and we were the conquering heroes. The plight of the Filipino people under the Japanese had been just as bad as that of the American POW.

One place in particular we visited was Mt. Oriat, the site where, on the first day of the war, Capt. Colin Kelly's plane crashed after being attacked by four Jap zeros. They shot into one of his oxygen tanks and it blew up, destroying his plane. He was able to get all of his crew out and everyone parachuted to safety. When he jumped out, the plane was falling apart and a wing hit and killed him. This was a very sad loss for those of us in the Philippine Islands, for Capt. Kelly was a great pilot and a true hero.

Another place of interest that we visited was the site where Gen. King surrendered to Gen. Homma. We spent time at Bataan, and we traveled the route of the Death March to Camp O'Donnell. We visited Capas and Cabanatuan. As we went along we all had different memories that we shared with each other. One man recalled, "This is where we spent the first night of the March. The Japanese guards searched us and our baggage. An officer from Albuquerque had a Japanese pistol in his bag which was found by one of the guards. They marched the officer over that hill and we never saw him again." As we continued another man spoke up, "This is where my buddy Joe fell and a Japanese guard bayoneted him. He never got up. I had to walk away and leave him there."

In one of the towns we went through we saw a tin warehouse. One of the men with us remembered spending the night there. He told us that the next morning the Japanese guards made the Filipino soldiers dig a grave for the men who had died during the night. One of the men was still alive and he kept trying to claw his way out, but the Japanese kept forcing the Filipinos to bury him. They were hesitant to do so, so the Japanese guard took a shovel and beat the American to death or at least unconscious. The Filipino soldiers then went on and buried him with the others that had died. The incidents were too many, and the memories too sad.

When we reached Capas we all recalled being jammed into boxcars for the long hot trip to Cabanatuan. We were in there so tight that the men that died were left upright because there was no place for them to fall.

Our next stop was Camp Cabanatuan. As we approached the entrance of the camp we could see there was one big difference. The fence posts were not the same. On our first trip to this camp we had been greeted with the sight of human heads on each fence post. As we walked through the camp we were all pretty quiet, almost as if we considered it to be holy ground.

After our trip through the Death March and Camp Cabanatuan we had plenty of time to visit and just sit around and have a bull session. Most of us had stories to tell and we all needed to get them out. Only those who had gone through the same experiences could really appreciate and understand. I have to admit that I gave thanks to the Lord for allowing me to survive the jaws of hell. When we left Ft. Bliss, Texas, in August of 1941, the 200th Coast Artillery (AA) was a full regiment consisting of 1,800 men. Now, four years later, less than 900 of our men were returning.

The eighteen days that I spent in Manila seemed like a very long time. We spent our days basking in the sun, watching the flying fish, and eating. We spent a lot of time just talking to each other. It was a wonderful feeling and we were all happy just to be free and do whatever we chose.

During this time we were treated to a couple of USO shows. It was so long ago that I can't remember the names of the actors or the singers and the dancers. There was a small hill where we all sat and the stage was below us. We truly enjoyed seeing the American performers. The comics must have been good because I remember laughing but I especially remember the girl dancers. These shows reminded us all of the loved ones we had waiting for us at home.

With the help of the Red Cross I was able to contact my wife and my family. Rose and Linda were now living in California with Rose's parents. I discovered that the only contact my family received from me during the time that I was a POW was a post card provided by the Red Cross. It had only a box to check off. I had checked off the box, "I am in good health." For most of the war they did not know if I was dead or alive.

On October 7, 1945, my daughter Linda celebrated her fifth birthday. I had not seen her since she was five months old. This was the first opportunity I had to wish her a happy birthday and I did so by wire. I let her know that I was well and of course very anxious to see her and her mother. There was no phone service between the Islands and the main land, so we could only communicate by letter or by wire.

Some of the men who were in the poorest of health had already been flown from Manila to San Francisco. We considered them lucky, but really those of us that were the healthiest were the lucky ones. Some of those boys were laid up in hospital beds for months, and a few never recovered. So, really, the lucky ones were those of us who were the healthiest.

In mid October we steamed out of Manila aboard the hospital ship USS *Mercy*. We were on our way to Pearl Harbor. Again, the mess hall was open twenty-four hours and we could order anything we wanted at anytime.

Figure 9-1: Hospital Ship, USS Mercy (AH-8)

When I was liberated at Camp Nomachi, I weighed less than 90 pounds. Forty-five days later at Fort Mason in San Francisco I weighed 165 pounds. It worked. The Army did fatten us up. We were glad that our families did not see us in the sad state we had been in at the time of our liberation.

When we arrived in Pearl Harbor we could see the remains of the attack of December 7, 1941. Little had been done to clean up the mess that the sneak attack by the Japanese had left. We did not have the time to visit Schofield Barracks or downtown Honolulu. The people we talked to told us of the damage that had been done to the Island, and of the large number of people that had been killed in the attack.

That evening, as we walked back to the ship, we were enjoying the wonderful beauty of Hawaii and understood why it is called Paradise. I was in Hawaii long enough to know that one day I would return with my wife to share the warm sunshine, the gentle rain, and the colors that make Hawaii the paradise that it is.

Back aboard the USS *Mercy*, we prepared to sail away from Oahu. We were sad to be leaving such beauty, but at the same time we were anxious to be going home to our families. As the ship left the harbor, I dropped my lei overboard and watched as it floated out of sight. Most of us stood on the deck just watching as the islands faded from view.

I have been fortunate enough to return to Hawaii with my wife on several occasions. It was a glorious feeling to visit not only Oahu but also the other islands. Each time that I visit I go to the USS *Arizona* Memorial. It is an eerie feeling to step aboard the memorial and know that so many sailors are still entombed inside the *Arizona* below.

About two or three days out of Hawaii in the middle of the Pacific, we ran into the tail end of a typhoon. It was a very sickening experience. Most of the men spent this time either in bed or hanging over the ship's railing. At times you could almost touch the water, and in the next few seconds you would look over the railing and it seemed the water was ten stories below. The typhoon caused us to lose fifteen precious hours. Finally, the great Pacific calmed down and we returned to the duty of the day. For us it was eating.

Some of the sailors aboard the USS *Mercy* were interested in hearing our stories. They wanted to know about our war experiences, our life in prison camp, and the treatment we had endured at the hand of the Japanese. It was hard then, as it is today, to recount some of our experiences. Only the men who had gone through the same things could understand and could believe the horror stories. We were advised to keep these horrible experiences to ourselves.

Welcome Home

It seemed like an eternity before we saw the beautiful Golden Gate Bridge. It was with great pride that we were returning to our beloved America. Pride in knowing that we fought for her, that many gave their lives for her, and to let the world know that we gave our blood, sweat, and tears for her. Our first sighting was of the large signs on the hillside overlooking the Pacific. They read "Welcome Home," "Job Well Done," "We Love You," "We Are Eternally Grateful." All of these signs were laid out on the hillsides of San Francisco so that we might read them as we sailed under the Golden Gate.

On the evening of October 26, 1945, we sailed into San Francisco Bay too late to dock because the tide was out. Most of us aboard ship were hugging the railing and looking at the San Francisco skyline, wishing we were there with our loved ones. We watched the little water taxis as they circled the ship. The people in the taxis strained to see if they could spot their men returning home from the war as we strained to see if we recognized a loved one. I knew that Rose and Linda would be on shore waiting for me. They were now living in the small community of Concord, California, just 40 miles outside of San Francisco. Rose had moved to California to work in the shipyards at Point Richmond. While I was a POW, my wife was doing her part to help with the war effort.

That night, the ship's crew had a movie for us. Even though we sat in the theater, no one was watching the movie. Too many thoughts were buzzing around our brains, each one of us wishing he could be ashore with family and friends.

It was hard to sleep that night. When it was time to get up, we were busy preparing to meet our loved ones. We were all busy showering, shaving, and getting ready to dock. During breakfast we were not very talkative. We were all deep in our own thoughts. How much had our loved ones changed? How much had we changed to them?

I don't remember what the breakfast consisted of that morning but I do remember that the cooks onboard fed us royally. We had the best of food and all we wanted. They did a great job of fattening us up.

We waited our turn to leave the ship. The litter cases, with men who needed to be carried off the ship, were the first to leave. Next to leave were the injured, like the ones on crutches or arms in a sling or injured in some other way. Those of us who were the healthiest waited until the last. My family was worried about me. This was a hospital ship and so many of the men leaving the ship seemed to be handicapped in some way.

Chapter 10: Homecoming

Rose and Linda

As I started down the gangplank, I spotted my wife Rose and my daughter Linda. *Would Linda come to me and let me hold her? Would she be shy and afraid of me?* So many thoughts as I scrambled down the gangplank. I stepped onto the dock and was greeted by relatives and friends, but I pushed through them to where Rose and Linda were. For five years, Rose and Linda were constantly on my mind. Now I finally had my baby girl and my wife in my arms. This was the greatest day of my life.

Figure 10-1: Linda and Rose Silva

On that day we were only allowed to spend a short time with our families. All too soon, we were rounded up and sent to Fort Mason for another complete physical. Those who were sick or injured remained in the hospital in Fort Mason. The healthy ones in my group were issued orders to leave at once and report to Birmingham General Hospital in Van Nuys, California. I spent that day on a train traveling down to southern California. I spent one night at Birmingham General, and the next day I was back on the train heading north.

I had a ten-day furlough and there was only one place where I wanted to spend it. I was in such a hurry to catch the next train north that I didn't stop to make a phone call.

I had several addresses and the train schedule with me. One of the cities listed on the train schedule was Oakland, California, and one of the addresses I had also said Oakland. It was the home of my aunt and uncle, Rachel[1] and Frank Romero. Uncle Frank had moved his family to California so he could work for the war effort. When I arrived in Oakland, I hailed a taxi again not taking the time to stop and make a phone call. The driver left me off in front of my aunt and uncle's home. My mother was in the front yard. I hurried into my mother's arms. We hugged, we kissed, and we cried. My mom and dad had come to California from New Mexico for my homecoming. They were staying at my Uncle Frank and Aunt Ray's home. I arrived that night just in time for dinner. This was the first dinner in almost five years that I was having with my parents, my aunt and uncle, and my cousins, the people I had grown up with. There was only one thing missing: my wife and my daughter were not with us. That same night, my cousin Eddie Romero drove me to Concord where Rose and Linda were living.

Figure 10-2: Rachel and Frank D. Romero

Uncle Frank and Aunt Ray had seven children. My cousin Pat Romero fought in Africa and Europe under Gen. George S. Patton. Pat retired as a major in the Army after 20 years of service. Bob and Ernie Romero were at Pearl Harbor when it was attacked. Bobby was in the Navy and stationed on a ship

---

1. Rachel (Raquela).

called the USS *Medusa*. On December 7, 1941, the USS *Medusa* took a direct hit from the Japanese and was sunk. He was able to swim to safety. Ernie was in the Coast Guard. His ship was also hit but did not sink. Both survived that December 7th attack. Frank Jr. served in the Army in the Pacific Theatre. The boys had an older half-brother, Phil Casias, who was also in the Army and fought in Europe. Eddie, and Charlie were too young to serve in World War II, and Betty was the youngest of the group.

The remainder of my furlough was spent between Concord and Oakland. Rose's sister and brother-in-law, Willie and Rita Garcia, also lived in Concord. Their home was large enough to provide Rose and me with a private bedroom. For most of that ten-day furlough, we stayed with them.

One thing about those ten days that stands out in mind is the box of letters that Rose gave to me. During the three and half years that I was a prisoner of the Japanese, my wife had sent to me numerous letters using the strict guidelines given to her by the U.S. War Department. All of the letters had been returned. This was my first opportunity to read my letters from home. I savored each word my wife had written.

At the end of my furlough I was sent back to Van Nuys where I spent about a month. Whenever the doctors at Birmingham would question me about my health I always told them I felt fine. I never mentioned the beriberi, malaria, dysentery or any other diseases I had suffered. If I could prove that I was fine, then maybe I would receive my discharge sooner.

My paternal grandmother, Dulcinea Berg Silva (December 7, 1879 – February 12, 1966) was living in Pasadena, California. Pasadena and Van Nuys are not too far from each other, so Rose and Linda moved in with my grandmother. I could hitch-hike from Van Nuys to Pasadena in no time at all. In 1945 it was not difficult for a man in uniform to hitch a ride to almost anywhere in this country. During my stay at Birmingham General, I spent every opportunity I had in Pasadena with my little family.

Figure 10-3: Dulcinea Berg Silva, circa 1945

I was sent from Van Nuys to Fort Bliss, Texas, in mid December 1945. In Fort Bliss, I spent most of my time in the barracks, or at the PX, or just reading. In those days there was no TV. We did have movies, and I remember one in particular, *They Were Expendable*, starring John Wayne, Robert Montgomery, and Ward Bond. This movie is about the fight to hold the Philippine Islands from the invading Japanese. It explains that our government had to make the choice to fight the war in Europe over the war in the Pacific. The men fighting in the Pacific Theater were expendable (designating equipment or men considered replaceable and therefore worth sacrificing to gain an objective). Even though our government considered us expendable, we still loved our country and we were all happy to be home.

Christmas 1945 was the most memorable Christmas of my life. I had a furlough from Fort Bliss, and a bus ticket to Albuquerque, New Mexico. In Albuquerque I met up with Rose who had come in by train from California. Together, we continued on to our hometown of Ratón. My parents were still living in Ratón, and Linda was also there. This was my first Christmas at home with my family in five years. Every Christmas decoration and every bite of my mother's home cooked Christmas feast was truly a dream come true. My dad had saved the barrels of first crush wine for the last four years in preparation for my homecoming. Family and friends celebrated that Christmas with delicious food and great wine.

I received an Honorable Discharge from the U.S. Army on April 4, 1946. Because I was stationed out of Fort Bliss, Texas, I was required to go there to pick up my discharge papers. Rose and my brother Henri accompanied me on this trip. To celebrate, we made plans to go out to dinner. In preparation for this dinner celebration, Rose went to the beauty parlor next to our hotel to get her hair done. She returned with a bag containing shampoo and curlers from the drug store. I asked her why she hadn't gotten her hair done at the beauty parlor. She then told me in a very distraught voice that she refused to go into the beauty parlor because of a sign in the window. The sign in the window read:

No dogs and no Mexicans allowed.

This kind of discrimination was so foreign to her that she refused to go into the beauty parlor and for the rest of her life she refused to return to the state of Texas.

Chapter 11: Civilian Life

Emotions

Soon after my discharge, I was asked to speak by an old friend of mine at a VFW (Veterans of Foreign Wars) meeting in Ratón. On the night of the meeting, I was picked up and driven to the VFW Hall. I was introduced to everyone there. I had known some of the men before the war. The meeting turned into a question and answer session, with me as the answer man. *Was it very bad in prison camp? Were the guards as vicious as we have heard? Did you see many men murdered on the Death March? Did the Japanese really behead people with their Samurai swords?* The questions that they asked were harder to answer than I had expected. Every question brought back memories, and for every memory I had to fight back my emotions.

After that experience, the principal of Ratón High School asked me to speak to the history class. I had to decline. I knew I couldn't take it and I also knew that I could never allow myself to speak about war experiences before a group again.

I decided that I needed to get my life in order, settle down, and enjoy my family. I now had time to enjoy my new life, my wife, and my daughter. The three of us went everywhere together. We traveled through the states of New Mexico, Colorado, Arizona, and California. I was trying to make up for all the lost years. My wife's parents were living in Concord, California, which is where Rose and Linda had also been living. Rose had been working as a welder in the shipyards in Point Richmond during the war. So, that is where we headed. Our second child, Penny, arrived on Linda's sixth birthday, October 7, 1946. Rose and I didn't waste any time adding to our family.

Figure 11-1: Rose, Vince, and Penny Silva

Work and Home

My first job was in an oil refinery. I was not happy there, so after a short time I quit and went to work in construction. This felt much better because I was getting something accomplished, building a home, a school, or just a garage. With construction, at least I had the satisfaction of seeing a finished product.

We soon purchased our first home in Concord, California. That is when I began to suffer from the awful nightmares. All the memories, all the atrocities and horrors that I was trying to repress during the day were manifesting themselves at night in the form of nightmares. The nightmares had both Rose and me very concerned.

Ex-POWs

It was after I became involved with the veteran's organization called the American Ex-Prisoners of War that the nightmares began to go away. Rose and I attended our first national convention in 1964 in Albuquerque, New Mexico. It seemed the perfect place to start this new organization of Ex-POWs. Most of the men of the 200th CA (AA) were from the state of New Mexico. This was a time when I could reunite and share stories with the only people that could understand, those that had experienced it with me.

Each year I would look forward to traveling with Rose to a different city for the annual Ex-POW convention. I found the conventions to be a place where I could openly discuss the horrors of war with men who understood. This proved to be a healing time for all of the members.

Figure 11-2: Vince and Rose at an Ex-POW Convention

Another group that proved to be very helpful to me was at the VA Clinic in Martinez, California. Each month a group of Ex-POWs would gather to share our stories of life as a POW. It was hard at first to speak about our experiences without breaking into tears. As the years progressed and we became stronger we did develop the ability to talk to each other about the war and remain calm. We could share our experiences without breaking down. No doctor, no hospital, and no family member could ever help us as much as we helped each other. We listened, we sympathized, and we understood.

Over the years I had lost contact with my two good friends from Camp Nomachi, the prison camp in Japan. One day in April 1986 when I was at the store, the phone rang at home. Rose answered and the voice on the other end asked her if she knew a Vince Silva who had been a prisoner of the Japanese in WWII. She told the man yes, that Vince Silva was her husband, and he had been a prisoner of the Japanese. He asked her if she knew the names of any of the men that were with him in the prison camp in Japan. Rose told him she did remember two names, one was Joder and one was Houser. He then told her, "I'm Dick Joder and I have been searching for Vince." He gave Rose his phone number and when I returned from the store I immediately called him. We had so much to talk about, so many memories. He told me that his doctor had told him he did not have long to live. He and his wife were living in Florida. Within a week I was on a plane to Florida. I spent the next two weeks visiting with my old buddy Dick Joder. We had gone through so much together. We had so many things to tell each other. Before I left Florida, Dick gave me an old leather pipe holder and a matching tobacco pouch, the same pipe holder and tobacco pouch that I had made in Camp Nomachi. I had given them to him back at prison camp, and now he was returning them to me. What a gift to go home with.

Figure 11-3: Leather pipe holder and matching tobacco pouch

Dick Joder passed away not long after that trip. I am so grateful I had those two weeks with him.

During one of the Ex-POW conventions I reunited with my old buddy Will Houser. We kept in touch until I received a call from his son several years ago. Will had just passed, and on his list of people to contact, my name and phone number were the first.

Recent Years

On Thanksgiving Day 2005, I celebrated 66 years of marriage with my wife Rose. During our years together we had five children, seven grandchildren, and eleven great-grandchildren. My youngest son Rick is no longer with us. He died from AIDS on October 7, 1991, at the age of 35. This was a very sad time for both my wife and me.

It was eight days after celebrating our 66th wedding anniversary that I lost the love of my life. Rose died of cancer on December 3, 2005. I am grateful for all the years and the large loving family that Rose and I had together.

I am writing this book so that my children and their children can pass it on. The stories, the memories, the horrors of WWII should not be forgotten.

Figure 11-4: Mema and Papa: Rose and Vincent Silva

Awards and Citations

The following are the awards and citations earned by SGT Vincent Silva during his service to our country from 15 March 1941 to 4 April 1946.

 Bronze Star

Heroic or meritorious achievement or service not involving participation in aerial flight.

 Purple Heart Medal

Awarded to any member of the U.S. Armed Forces killed or wounded in an armed conflict. See "1996 National Defense Authorization Act" on page A-58.

 Prisoner of War Medal

Awarded to any member of the U.S. Armed Forces taken prisoner during any armed conflict dating from World War I.

 Army Good Conduct Medal

Exemplary conduct, efficiency and fidelity during three years of active enlisted service with the U.S. Army (one year during wartime).

 American Defense Service Medal (WWII)

U.S. Army: Twelve months of active duty service during 1939-41.

    American Theatre Campaign Medal

Service outside the U.S. in the American theater for 30 days or within the continental U.S. for one year.

Asiatic Pacific Campaign Medal (WWII)

Service in the Asiatic-Pacific theater for 30 days or receipt of any combat decoration.

World War II Victory Medal

Awarded for service in U.S. Armed Forces between 1941 and 1946.

Philippine Defense Medal

Service in defense of the Philippines between 8 December 1941 and 15 June 1942.

Philippine Liberation Medal

Service in the liberation of the Philippines between 17 October 1944 and 3 September 1945.

Philippine Independence Medal

Receipt of both Philippine Defense & Liberation Medals/Ribbons. Originally presented to those present for duty in the Philippines on 4 July 1946.

New Mexico Special MacArthur Service (Bataan Medal)

Awarded to those who were assigned to the 200th Coast Artillery (C.A.) and served under General Douglas MacArthur in the Philippines on 7 December 1941.

U.S. Presidential Unit Citation

Philippine Presidential Unit Citation

 **WWII Honorable Discharge**

Combat Infantryman Badge

1996 National Defense Authorization Act

SEC. 521. AWARD OF PURPLE HEART TO PERSONS WOUNDED WHILE HELD AS PRISONERS OF WAR BEFORE APRIL 25, 1962. (a) Award of Purple Heart.--For purposes of the award of the Purple Heart, the Secretary concerned (as defined in section 101 of title 10, United States Code) shall treat a former prisoner of war who was wounded before April 25, 1962, while held as a prisoner of war (or while being taken captive) in the same manner as a former prisoner of war who is wounded on or after that date while held as a prisoner of war (or while being taken captive). (b) Standards for Award.--An award of the Purple Heart under subsection (a) shall be made in accordance with the standards in effect on the date of the enactment of this Act for the award of the Purple Heart to persons wounded on or after April 25, 1962. (c) Eligible Former Prisoners of War.--A person shall be considered to be a former prisoner of war for purposes of this section if the person is eligible for the prisoner-of-war medal under section 1128 of title 10, United States Code.

Figure A-1: Receiving the Purple Heart

Brig. Gen. Kenny C. Montoya of the New Mexico National Guard presented the Purple Heart to SGT Vincent Silva, April 9, 2006, in Santa Fé, New Mexico. Gen. Montoya is a native of Ratón, New Mexico, and took great pleasure and pride in presenting the medal to one of his own hometown soldiers. Gen. Montoya's maternal grandparents, Willie and Florence Martinez, were "compadres" of Vince's parents.

Family Tree

The following page show graphical representations of Vincent Silva's family. Information was gathered using several sources such as the following:

- Santa Clara Catholic Church, Wagon Mound, NM – baptismal certificates
- Sacred Heart Catholic Church, Watrous, NM – baptismal certificates
- Holy Trinity Catholic Church, Trinidad, CO – baptismal certificates
- New Mexico Genealogical Society

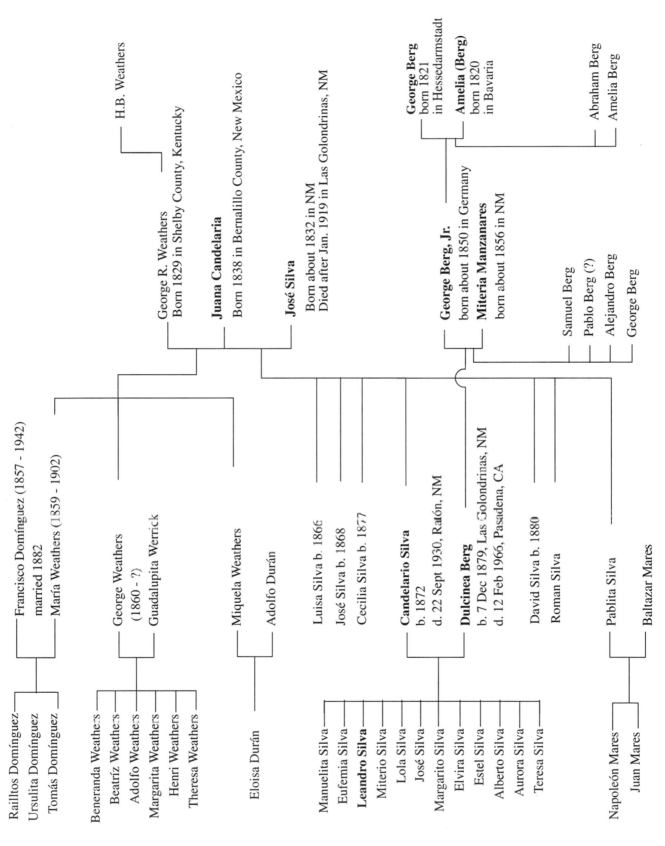

Figure B-1: Ancestors and Relatives of Leandro (Lee) Silva

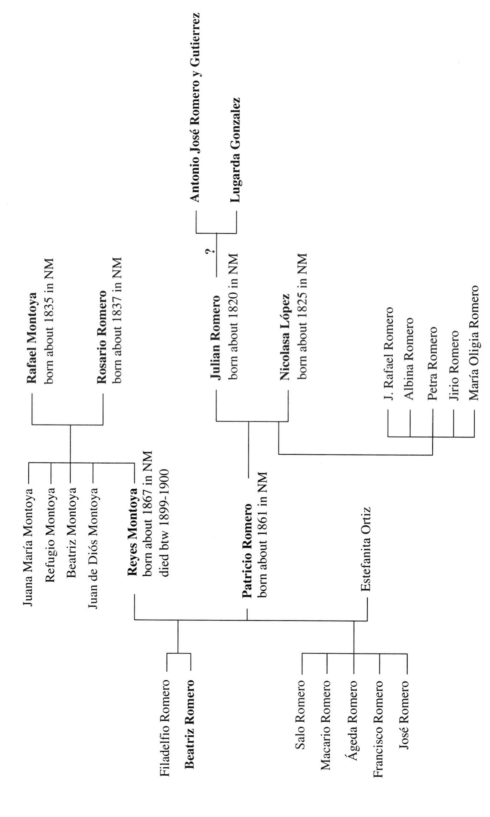

Figure B-2: Ancestors and Relatives of Beatriz (Beatrice) Romero Silva

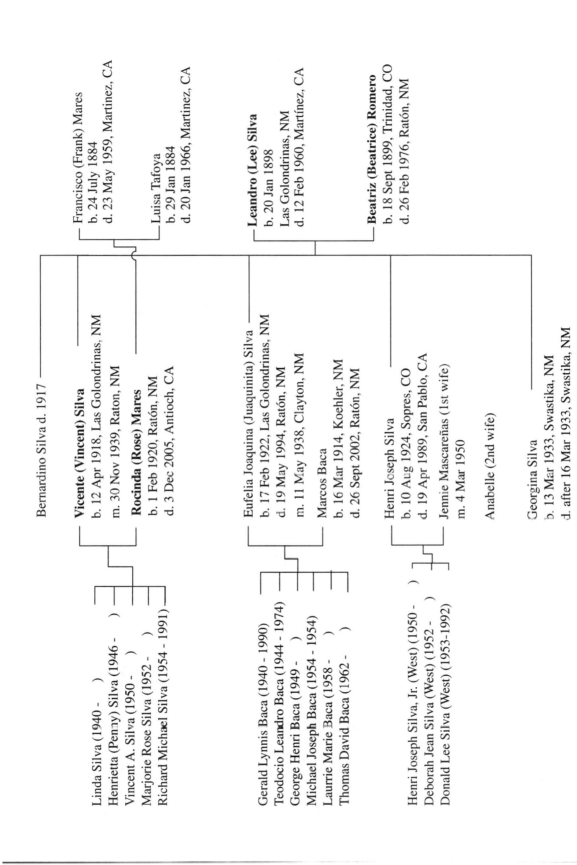

Bernardino Silva d. 1917

Francisco (Frank) Mares
b. 24 July 1884
d. 23 May 1959, Martinez, CA

Luisa Tafoya
b. 29 Jan 1884
d. 20 Jan 1966, Martinez, CA

Leandro (Lee) Silva
b. 20 Jan 1898
Las Golondrinas, NM
d. 12 Feb 1960, Martínez, CA

Beatriz (Beatrice) Romero
b. 18 Sept 1899, Trinidad, CO
d. 26 Feb 1976, Ratón, NM

Vicente (Vincent) Silva
b. 12 Apr 1918, Las Golondrinas, NM
m. 30 Nov 1939, Raton, NM

Rocinda (Rose) Mares
b. 1 Feb 1920, Ratón, NM
d. 3 Dec 2005, Antioch, CA

Eufelia Joaquina (Juaquinita) Silva
b. 17 Feb 1922, Las Golondrinas, NM
d. 19 May 1994, Ratón, NM
m. 11 May 1938, Clayton, NM

Marcos Baca
b. 16 Mar 1914, Koehler, NM
d. 26 Sept 2002, Ratón, NM

Henri Joseph Silva
b. 10 Aug 1924, Sopres, CO
d. 19 Apr 1989, San Pablo, CA

Jennie Mascareñas (1st wife)
m. 4 Mar 1950

Anabelle (2nd wife)

Georgina Silva
b. 13 Mar 1933, Swastika, NM
d. after 16 Mar 1933, Swastika, NM

Linda Silva (1940 -   )
Henrietta (Penny) Silva (1946 -   )
Vincent A. Silva (1950 -   )
Marjorie Rose Silva (1952 -   )
Richard Michael Silva (1954 - 1991)

Gerald Lynnis Baca (1940 - 1990)
Teodocio Leandro Baca (1944 - 1974)
George Henri Baca (1949 -   )
Michael Joseph Baca (1954 - 1954)
Laurrie Marie Baca (1958 -   )
Thomas David Baca (1962 -   )

Henri Joseph Silva, Jr. (West) (1950 -   )
Deborah Jean Silva (West) (1952 -   )
Donald Lee Silva (West) (1953 - 1992)

Figure B-3: Descendents of Lee and Beatrice Silva

Figure B-4: Candelario Silva, father of Lee Silva

Figure B-5: Dulcinea Berg Silva (Grandma Candy), mother of Lee Silva

Figure B-6: Patricio Romero, father of Beatrice Romero Silva

Figure B-7: Reyes Montoya Romero, mother of Beatrice Romero Silva

Figure B-8: Lee and Beatrice (Romero) Silva circa 1916

Figure B-9: Lee and Beatrice (Romero) Silva circa 1948

Figure B-10: Rose Mares Silva on her wedding day, November 30, 1939

Figure B-11: Vincent Silva on his wedding day, November 30, 1939

Poems by Vincent Silva

Among his many passions – family, country, education, reading (until he lost his eye sight) – Vincent wrote poetry. We have selected a few of the many poems he has written through the years to include in his book.

- "The Death March" tells the story of how a group of surrendered American soldiers happen upon the body of one of their comrades. The body of the young soldier has one arm pointing into the distance. As they pass, they wonder to where he's pointing.

- "The Defenders of Bataan" relates the discussion between the devil and St. Peter regarding the soldiers of Bataan and how nothing could crush their spirit.

- "Why Do I Weep" gives us a mere glimpse of the anguish and helplessness Vince endured seeing so many of his comrades perish on the Death March and in the prisoner of war camps.

- "Our Last Goodbye" was written in memory of Vince's youngest son Rick.

- "To Those I Love" conveys Vince's gratitude to his family and friends for the years of love they shared and how he, when he leaves us, will wait for us on the other side.

The Death March

'Twas the morning of the surrender.
We were trooping o'r the hill.
The sound of tired marching feet
Broke the unaccustomed still.

When we came upon a soldier
Just a youth not yet a man.
He had left his home in New Mexico
To fight in old Bataan.

Where are you pointing soldier?
What message would you give?
What are you trying to tell us,
The ones who are left to live?

Do you point to a place called home
That lies beyond the sea?
Where family and friends await you
But you never again will see?

Or do you point to where you have gone
To that distant Golden Shore?
Where man can live like brothers
Where there isn't any war?

We must march on and leave you now
Just a pile of flesh and bone.
We know not where we are going
Our fate may be worse than your own.

In future years when a maddened world
Is ready to fight again
Let's all remember that up-raised arm.
Let's heed its message then.

The Defenders Of Bataan

When the Gates of Hell are open well
And the devil does all he can,
There sit those souls upon the coals,
The Defenders of Bataan.

Then the devil goes high into the sky
To interview Saint Pete,
He's full of charm in his uniform;
His horns are all shiny and neat.

"Saint Pete," says he, "How can it be?
Those souls have called my bluff.
I've turned the heat up to its peak,
But they are much too tough.

"They won't brown or even frown,
Nor ask for the water can.
What can I do with such a crew
The Defenders of Bataan?"

"I surmise," says Pete, while looking wise,
"Those souls have called your bluff.
You've turned the heat up to its peak
But they are much too tough.

"It's plain to see you must give to me
Their keeping at this point,
For they fought well while in that Hell
And now deserve this joint."

Why Do I Weep

Why do I weep? Why do I cry
When I think of my comrades and the way that they died?
How do I erase the horrors of war?
How do I forget what I went through before?

I remember the lad that cried out in pain,
"Mama, dear Mama, please help me again."
So many of my comrades on the Death March did die.
So tell me please, why shouldn't I cry?

The number of men buried at O'Donnell per day.
I wept for them then and I still cry today.
There were a lot of heroes in the jungles of Bataan.
They deserve to be remembered and to be mentioned again

'Cause history doesn't tell us why we lost so many men.
Please ignore me if I weep.
Please forgive me when I cry.
For I still see all my comrades that in prison camp did die.

Our Last Goodbye

As I sit here in the twilight
And the day is nearly done,
I cannot help but ponder
As I watch the setting sun,

On my son now gone forever
Who was taken in his prime
By a sickness of this world
And by age old Father Time.

We had him for a while,
And we are grateful this is true;
We thank you, heavenly Father;
Now we send him back to you.

Our sorrow is enormous;
To bear it we will try;
Family and friends are gathered today
To bid our last goodbye.

To Those I Love

When I am gone, please let me go.
Don't tie yourself to me with tears.
I have so much I need to do.
Be happy we had all the many years.

I gave you my love. And you can only guess
How much you gave me in happiness.
I thank you all for the love you've shown.
Now it's time for me to travel alone.

So grieve awhile for me if you must.
Then let your grief be comforted by trust.
Keep all the memories within your heart.
It's only briefly that we must part.

And if you find you need me, I'll be here.
Not seen or heard, I'll still be near.
You'll feel my love if you listen with your heart;
For all of you, I'll still be a great big part.

When it's your turn to come this way;
Then you will know I've held you close day after day;
For I will greet you with a great big smile.
And I will say, "Welcome home, my child!"

Additional Information

This appendix contains additional information and photos such as the following:

- Family photo Christmas 1977
- Instructions for families on how to contact prisoners of war.
- Story by Anthony Silva, Vincent's grandson.

Figure D-1: Rose and Vince with their children Rick, Marjorie, Vince Jr., Penny, and Linda

15 October 1943

REVISED JAPANESE MAILING INSTRUCTIONS

PRISONER OF WAR INFORMATION BUREAU
OFFICE OF THE PROVOST MARSHAL GENERAL

WASHINGTON, 25, D. C.

The Provost Marshal General, being charged with the responsibility of furnishing all available information concerning American Prisoners of War, has directed that the following information be given to every interested person.

When a member of the armed forces of the United States has been officially reported interned as a prisoner of war by the Japanese Government ordinary mail may be sent, postage free, through regular postal channels by relatives and friends. It is not necessary to send prisoner of war mail to this office for forwarding. You are also advised not to attempt to correspond with a member of our armed forces whom you believe to be held as a prisoner of war until you have first determined his official status from this Bureau because only those letters which are addressed to officially reported prisoners of war will be permitted to go forward by the Postal Censor.

The importance of correctly addressing prisoner of war mail cannot be too strongly emphasized. In this connection, The International Red Cross, Geneva, Switzerland, has reported as follows:

"Among the 100,000 messages received in Tokyo, more than 700 letters addressed to American and British prisoners of war could not reach their destination because the addresses were not sufficiently clear.

The Japanese authorities have created a special post office, connected with the prisoners of war camp in Tokyo, which is in charge of distribution of mail to prisoners. The staff of this post office is composed of American and British officers. These officers point out that the insufficient addresses make it difficult, if not impossible, to forward these letters. The name and first name are not enough; there may be a few prisoners of the same name. Besides, these prisoners of war with similar names are often interned in camps many hundred miles apart".

Strict adherence to the instructions in this circular will facilitate censoring and the ultimate delivery of prisoner of war mail.

When addressing prisoner of war mail, the rank, complete name (including the middle initial or middle name), prisoner of war number (when known) and place of internment or camp number (when known) shall be used.

The face of the envelope should be prepared as follows when the place of internment is not known:

Prisoner of War Mail   Postage Free

(Insert Rank and Complete Name here),
American Prisoner of War, (# when known),
c/o Japanese Red Cross,
Tokyo, Japan,
Via: New York, New York.

24-55025A8CD

A+

"PAPA"

by

Anthony Silva

Age 11

October 17, 1984

Hold Shelf Slip

All Contra Costa County Libraries will be
closed Sunday, April 8th. Book drops will
remain open. Materials can be renewed online
at ccclib.org or by phone at 800-984-4636

Item Number 31901048587796

JOHNSON CAREN GAY

4/12/2012

...call "Papa", was born April
...orthern New Mexico named Mora.
... 1,000 acres. His family raised
...ad many chores on the ranch,
...so the horses that they used

... Mares, on Thanksgiving day in
... Their first child, my aunt Linda,
...n that same year, he joined the
... Clark Field on Luzon Island in

...er the bombing of Pearl Harbor,
...d. My Papa was eventually cap-
...risoner of the Japanese until
...and one half years.
...can X-POW's, the Disabled Ameri-
...nders of Bataan and Corregidor.
...ce, my aunt Linda was about one
... freed by the Japanese and came

...In 1950 my father Vincent was
...rn, and in 1955 my uncle Rick
..., seven grandchildren and two

My Papa has ... st of his life and has made me
many things. A bird house, many shelves, stools to stand on, a picnic
table, and benches and many other things.

My Papa is now retired and he and my Mema have recently moved
to Albuquerque, New Mexico. I am hoping to visit them soon.

I love them and I always will love them.

Index

Numerics

A

B

C

D

E

Printed in the United States
104884LV00001B/201-454/P

3 1901 04858 7796